Five Gifts That Shaped My Life
BEST GIFTS EVER

- Samar Deep Singh

PUBLISHED BY:

Gurucool Publishing
#102, Sai Krupa Nilayam,
Nagendra Nagar,
Habsiguda, Hyderabad – 500007

Ph: 040–69999200

E-mail: info@gurucoolpublishing.com

© Samar Deep Singh (Author)

First Edition – 2019

ISBN: 978-93-88435-34-5

Price: INR 190/-

Laser typesetting by	: Ms. Ananya G., Hyderabad
Cover page photo	: Pixabay, Creative Commons
Cover Design by	: Majestic Designs, Hyderabad
Printed at	: Devanshi Digital Printers, Hyderabad

PREFACE

Childhood is the best phase of our life. Grandparents make it awesome and special. Lucky are those who spend ample time with them. Their lessons and valuable insight about life enrich our thoughts. They are truly our best teachers.

This book is a tribute to the sweet and cosy relationship between grandparents and their little devils. It consists of short stories for every age-group that will surely remind you of childhood memories.

Ron finds valuable life lessons in Dadu's (grandfather) bedtime stories and thrilling adventures. It helps him in attaining success and dealing with relationships. Hope the readers will love and enjoy every part of it.

 Utmost care has been taken to make the book error-free by the author and the editor. Please forgive us and let us know to make it error-free. This book comprises two other parts.

'Crazy stupid classmates' & 'Ron and the secret society of ghosts' that will be available shortly.

Your comments and feedback are most welcome.

Let's celebrate childhood.

Samar deep singh

samardeepsingh1075@gmail.com

New Delhi

1.10.2019

Acknowledgements

At first, a special thanks to Dr Vineet Gera for motivating me to follow my passion for writing. Sir, I am truly indebted to you for the active support and guidance to make this book possible.

A big thanks to the editor Mrs Pranitha Oswin. You took larger than the life efforts in the editing process of the book.

To my Wife – Jashmi Deep Singh; thanks for tolerating me. Your constant support and encouragement made it possible in a very short time. Discussing with you about the stories along with a cup of coffee were the days that I would cherish whole my life.

I am lucky to have such an efficient team of Gurucool publishers that made this effort a cakewalk.

Deepest gratitude to my friends and colleagues for constant encouragement and support. Let me mention all of you –

Prashant Kumar Chaudhary (JCB), Ranjit Kadam (NDMC), Munna Yadav (NTPC), Saurabh Verma (NTPC), Pankaj Kumar(AAI), Rashmi Narain (BOB), Rakesh Koli (IAF) & Sumit Kumar (UPL).

A big thanks to the readers who accepted my work. Please feel free to send your valuable reviews and feedback about the book. This would make me a better author.

Samar deep Singh

New Delhi

Samar1075@yahoo.com

www.pennedbysamar.com

To

Jashmi
&
Samara

Let me introduce myself to you

Dear friends. I'm Ron. I would like to thank the author for choosing me as a Hero of this book. But, my grandfather - nicknamed 'Dadu' was the real one. We are a family of British Descent but decided to reside in India at Dehradun, after independence.

To nickname a person was quite an Indian thing, irrespective of age or gender. Originally, I was named as 'Rohan' at birth by my beloved parents. But, it was later changed to Ron due to my British connections. I owe it to my neighbours and school friends.

Dadu was a wing commander at Indian Air Force and had an adventurous career. My father was a Chartered Accountant but got promoted within a decade as the CEO of an Industrial firm at a reputed MNC. My mother was a clerk at a reputed PSU Bank. Both were quite busy at their respective careers.

Two events shaped my destiny and it was quite a U-turn of my life.

At first, I was rusticated from the boarding school. They were not able to handle my mischiefs and pranks.

Later on, I took admission at St. Mary's public school nearby my home. My woes in the study continued until I met Dadu.

Next, It was the Dadu's retirement. Sometimes, I think that God had sent him to me. Our friendship grew stronger with time.

I was fortunate to partner with him in a series of daring adventures filled with mystery and thrill. The bedtime stories told by him were equally awesome and had the same genre. Come and explore them with me.

Table of Contents

MAGNIFYING GLASS
The First Gift

The greatest magnifying glasses in the world are a man's own eyes when they look upon his own person.

- Alexander pope

1. Getting closer to Santa

2. Cracking the Glass Museum Code
3. The secret of Robber's cave
4. Corporate student

1. Getting closer to Santa

27th December 2000

Dehradun

The Christmas had just sneaked out. My Santa still evaded me. I remembered the pot-bellied priest's voice at the Shiva temple - Only goddess Laxmi visits India at Diwali. But, I was pretty sure that being a bona fide student of St. Mary's public school; Santa must visit me. At a brisk pace, I was heading towards Dadu's room, with a great burden in my heart and in search of Santa. My dearest Grandfather was nicknamed as 'Dadu'.

"Would Dadu be my Santa?" -- I thought for a second.

But, I refuted myself as Dadu's silky white beard had more resemblance to Professor Dumbledore rather than that of Santa. I proudly styled myself as Mr Harry potter. My conscience just spat out more honestly as my classmates didn't even dub me as Mr Ron Weasley or rather a rat.

Meanwhile, the cold Dehradun night had already reddened my cheeks.

But, my shivering heart was still spiralling with numerous questions as quickly as an ice-cream melts in the summer. The old memories again wetted my conscience.

I was always special to my 'Dadu', even though the whole class dubbed me as a miserable failure, including my parents.

Finally, I decided to enter Dadu's room.

Maybe! I could find Santa hidden somewhere inside the room to surprise me.

The pin-drop silence was disturbed by a slow, but continuous sound of snoring. Any hope of surprise had dashed. Santa didn't pop up. But, a smiling Buddha kept beside the table welcomed me.

 A dim light of night bulb lit the room. It helped me define the assets placed in the room - two tables placed side by side across the cupboard, one almirah & a bed on which Dadu was sleeping could be traced with ease.

Every prominent moment of Dadu's life was depicted on the four walls of the room. At the extreme corner, Dadu was holding a baby. Everyone recognized that baby as me. "How can I be so small?" I always questioned myself and refuted that resemblance as me.

Once, when I refuted this in front of the Priest who visited dadu's room, had said pointing towards me - That's how an atheist refutes the existence of God. I smiled in surprise, having no idea about the priest's kind words.

I remembered that Dadu once said – "collect memories, not assets".

Ron's Best Gifts ever – samar deep singh

Likely, it was the same motto that had chiselled the interiors of Dadu's room! Evidently, the memories exceeded luxuries in his life that was pretty evident in his room. My eyes gazed at Dadu's face for a moment & my heart had compared him with that of my father's.

Both of them seemed like two rugged mountains separated by a trench. My mother always nicknamed it as 'generation – gap'. I consider myself as a hill at the side of Dadu and still not separated by any trench. Even, that hill always had got the taste of melting snow of Dadu's mountain i.e. the love.

On the table, I saw the five precious gifts that Dadu had gifted me on my consecutive birthdays. My father, while sending me to a boarding school, deserted me with that stuff & to the worse; the Dadu himself.

One piece of advice that I still remember; that was quite swiftly spoken by Dadu - simplicity comes with unknown mysteries; it's upon us as to how we unravel their

 significance or deep hidden meaning inside it.

Being a part-time teacher; after his retirement from the Indian Air Force, he had developed a unique style of teaching by which anyone could understand except my father. He simply took wheat flour, cream, chocolate chips, bread and made my favourite black forest cake. That's how I got that concept.

Good heavens!

Alas! I wished that my teachers could have followed this simple trick. I started to slowly touch and feel all my gifts lying on the table like a curious blind reading the 'Braille Script'. How simply the gifts of Dadu touched my heart, much more than that of my parents & classmates! A stupid smile touched my face while recollecting all in my mind.

The first thing that I had noticed was an 'Hourglass' -a simple one though; given by him on my ninth birthday. It had two glass bulbs connected vertically through a narrow neck.

A considerable amount of sand trickles from one bulb to another, under the effects of gravity. Dadu had fixed radium wires around it, later on. It resembled the sand dancing amidst the group of stars.

The Magnifying glass was gifted on my tenth birthday. That year, I had failed in all the subjects. When I scanned it on an ant or any other insect; it got bigger surprisingly. Once, Dadu had burnt a paper, while putting it between paper & the sun. It was surely able to surpass Mr Harry Potter's magic wand in real life.

A set of coloured pebbles was gifted on my eleventh birthday. It was quite funny. Whenever I put them in any hollow box & shook it, the sound got dearer to me. It was quite mesmerizing to me. But, it irritated my father.

Mirror- It was gifted on my twelfth birthday, it was very special to me. A round frame housed five different sets of mirrors. One showed your own real image. One of them showed the bulged image & another in a smaller size. The other two showed concave & convex images, respectively. With it, I used to make fun of others. It depicts not to take life seriously.

Violin- It was a musical instrument given by him on my thirteenth birthday. That year, I was sent to the boarding school. So, I was in little connection with it.

Suddenly, the Hourglass slipped on the ground from the table as I flipped it quite hard & it touched the carpet. The sound had awakened Dadu. Five years had passed since we met.

"Who's this?"-Dadu asked in surprise & wore his spectacles simultaneously.

"Ron, my son! You have come after a very long time!" He asked in surprise.

I burst into tears immediately, as if it were eager to evaporate through some words of wisdom. Dadu hugged me at once. Thanks to the monster called Generation- Gap.

Dadu had always poured two streams of love into my heart. One stream was of my father's & the other one was of the Dadu himself.

"What happened, my dear? Are you crying?" He asked me.

I exploded into another sea of emotions.

"Dadu! There is nothing much left in my life. I am finished now.

"I wanna die." I lamented.

My rolling tears were the questions drenched into the mist of innocence.

My heart hoped that Dadu would be the answer to all my sorrows, and would end my periods of depression. Not every one of us can cry our heart out to anyone. It needs an able shoulder.

 Dadu smiled a little & said - "One day we all will! But, we have to play our innings with passion. Everyone will retire one day or the other into infinity. Success and failure are just the two sides of a coin. The importance lies in how you earn that coin". Dadu enlightened me further.

I gazed at Dadu's face,but I was still confused about what he said.

"I don't understand". I told him at once.

"Just sleep and take a rest for now. We will talk in the morning". Dadu said after patting me lightly.

The two souls now slept together. The generation gap had melted away. Love, the purest emotion on this earth has overtaken the periods of depression, anxiety & despair from my heart.

Had my Santa arrived finally? I thought for a while.

A shoulder of maturity had nestled an immature soul of innocence this time. That's how the law of nature works. A layer of experience cuddles another layer of immaturity; so that the bees of immaturity can absorb the nectar of experience.

Evidently, Santa was just a misnomer as I forgot him while melting into Dadu's arms.

2. Cracking the Glass Museum code

Every student knew about the majestic 'Glass museum'.

It was not the venue of a typical 'boring' Olympiad that opens annually for the intelligent students nor a 'Mensa test' designed for individuals having higher intelligence quotient.

The Glass Museum was the structure built of tempered transparent glass housed above the hill , abutting the vast seashore. When you enter the premises; multiple reflections of numerous mirrors cause your image displayed all over the museum.

Its interior was built by using lakhs of mirrors to reflect the images. In addition, the beautiful glass work gave it the title of a 'masterpiece'. The audio-visual screens add life to the museum.

But, unfortunately a common visitor could only visit its outer façade & limited floors. To explore it completely, one has to answer a puzzle at every level.

On completion of all the levels, a certificate of merit & a Gold medal was given to the winner. It was presumed as the most prestigious award that can make you a celebrity overnight.

Only a Genius could complete all the levels & thus, could explore the whole premises. The success rate is only one per cent. I have tried thrice but failed in all the attempts. Lastly, it was two years back that I tried it with one of my best friends.

At the entrance, the guard offered us the rules brochure. Let me make you familiar with some of them.

- A. The competition has six levels with an exit gate, in case of failure at any level.
- B. An Hourglass having two glass bulbs connected vertically with a narrow neck to measure the passage of time was given to the participants. If the lower bulb gets filled by the trickling sand fully, it indicates that your time's up.
- C. You can join the competition with another companion of your choice.
- D. One chance per year for a participant.

Rest of the rules were to maintain discipline & decorum at the premises. Every school principle could be seen chanting such rules, causing them too common & familiar to repeat here again.

Let's come to the point now. At the first level, the Robot at the entrance showed us two paths. Only one path had to be chosen out of the two. We chose the path that was welcomed by the fairies. We got disqualified & reached the exit gate. The Display Board at the exit reads:

"Take a selfie, you Morons and better luck next time."

It was a matter of grave insult for both of us. It had become a top-secret between me & my best friend since then. We have never told about our visit to anyone.

On my next attempt, I approached the museum with my mother.

Again, at level one it showed two paths; one having a red background and another with a pink one. Her favourite colour was pink & she was dressed up so. Pink from head to toe except for the silky black hair. Her fascination with the pink colour had failed me this time as she had chosen the pink background.

We got disqualified at first level itself. But, the display board was a little kind to us this time. The display board showed no insulting comments. Moreover, we got two apples & a bottle of juice at the exit gate.

On another attempt, I persuaded a topper of my class to accompany me. Again, two paths appeared to us. One with the simple questions of maths & another with the questions of GK. He chose the first immediately and failed again.

I messaged this breaking news to my school friends titled – 'Topper had failed'.

This spicy news spread to the whole school like fire. It affected his reputation badly. Toppers can top everywhere….the myth was broken.

It was a pleasant Sunday. I talked about the 'Glass Museum' to Dadu.

"I am too dumb to solve the puzzles at the Glass museum," I said in a low tone.

"You are quite an intelligent boy. You will solve it one day. Keep trying" Dadu said to me.

Next week, we flew to our destination at the heart of the Nicobar Islands.

A fat guard welcomed us at the reception.

"I knew you well. You are a frequent visitor at level one" He said & laughed a bit.

Dadu smiled at him too.

"At least he tried!" Dadu told him frankly in my defense.

The guard handed over an hourglass to us.

"Do you need another rules brochure?" He said, smiling at me.

I denied instantly seeking the possibility of another round of insults by him.

Please follow the instructions at the Display board & the Robot at each level. I shared my previous experiences with Dadu.

We entered our battleground. Two paths were in front of us. One with a black background, having an armchair at the centre & an ice-cream shop at the corner. The other one had a rugged path full of stones & skeletons.

"Dadu, we have got another chance to enjoy an ice-cream pact for free at path one" I exclaimed with joy.

"Hmmm! Then it will fetch you another apple with a chance to get a selfie at the exit" He told me dashing all my excitement to doom.

"Ron! The path to success is hard at the beginning. It demands sacrifices. An easy one or comfortable way will get you nowhere". Dadu enlightened me a bit.

"We chose the rugged path with stones "I yelled to the Robot at the screen to tick my choice.

The display board read..."Congrats you have qualified level one."   The path having an armchair & ice – cream shop got disappeared within a second. My joy knew no bounds.

"Wow! Dadu; you have done it. You are my hero. The rugged path was just an illusion with a 3 -D effect. That one was also quite comfortable. Now I could proudly say that at least I have crossed the level one" I yelled with joy.

"Ron! The path with an armchair & an ice-cream shop was a trap. It was created to mislead you. If we stick to our comforts and favourites, then success will never touch us" Dadu enlightened me further.

We cut the congratulatory ribbon at the entrance of next level. It was quite a celebrity experience.

Now, you can stop your hourglass & enjoy along the poolside - a display popped up at the screen at our right side.

"Sure!" Dadu replied in a proud tone.

The pool had three cute dolphins. I enjoyed playing volleyball with them.

It's the time for level two. A Robot popped up on the screen again. Within a few minutes, another screen displayed all the superheroes, including 'ourselves' at the centre. They were spiderman, superman etc., with all my favourite cartoons characters lined up on the screen one after the other.

The hourglass sand was drifting away to its lower bulb with gravity. Time flies. Its minute particles of sand were equivalent to the second hand of the electronic clock. Time has got modern, but it remained the same....I thought for a second.

"Dadu! We should choose Spidey. It could help us with his webs" I Said.

He looked at me and chose quite differently opposite to that of my choice.

Dadu told the Robot. "We will choose ourselves. We don't need any superheroes. We are the heroes of our own destiny."

"Had Dadu committed a blunder? Alas! Time has come for our elimination "I thought for a while.

But the Robot yelled the opposite that surprised me again.

"You have won "The screen flashed for a second to congratulate us.

A car came towards us having a trail of tracks.

Good heavens!

It was a roller coaster ride at first. Then; it rode us into a tunnel by which we could watch the bottom of the sea. The whole tunnel was covered with glass panels by which we could view the interior of the sea. It showed us multiple coloured fishes, octopus, hydras etc. apart from the species having colourful scales & bodies.

A shark also passed by us. It was an awesome experience.

"Why didn't you choose any superhero? "I asked Dadu impatiently.

"My dear son, People waste time in following the path of others. We should create our own. We should believe in ourselves".....He said with a smile on his face.

Now it's the time for the third level. The Robot popped up again at our extreme left side, which showed us the images of my classmates and five old people.

You have to choose any one of them and that person will accompany you to make your task easier"...the Robot told us.

I found myself a bit unlucky here. They were the classmates that I hated the most. So, I told Dadu to decide as per his own choice.

"None, from my side too!" ---- Dadu told me.

So, I told the Robot in a proud voice that I have already chosen my Dadu & I don't need anyone.

"Why didn't you choose from any of your classmates?" Dadu asked me.

"I disliked all of them". I replied to him in a low tone.

"Why didn't you choose your mates, Dadu?"I asked him impatiently.

"All of them had died. So, how would they come to help us?"

"It was another trap. Moreover, we should try to walk alone in our path of the journey" said Dadu.

Another Robot popped up from our right side.

"Congrats! You have won another level."

"Really! Fortune favours the brave" I thought for a second.

The gate opened to the Jacuzzi bath & the lunch. Two assistants came up to help us. We had our gala time.

Now, the fourth level was waiting for us. A peculiar sound disturbed us. "Attention you are about to enter a cave.

The cave is full of bats & mysterious birds. It may harm you. You can take any of the arms kept in the box placed on your left side to tackle them."

I saw a Bow, Mace, Gun, etc., in the box on my left side.

"Ron! What is your skill?" Dadu asked again in a low tone.

It's my catapult. I am adept at it. I always keep it with myself. We broke a sandstone rock with a mace & got some pieces with ourselves.

"We would not take any of the arms here. I will use my own skill ."We informed the Robot.

We entered the cave further. I downed many bats with my catapult that came our way.

We reached the end of the cave. Underneath, there was complete water. We saw two sets of apparatus on our right side. We wore them.

"Ah! It's a scuba diving costume" Dadu told me. He looked quite curious this time.

We waded into the waters. An amazing experience of sea life was awaiting us. Vibrant fishes, awesome coral bodies, sea urchins, an octopus just passed nearby us.

It was a perfect holiday experience.

We now entered into some sort of a jungle as the shore had come. We left the scuba diving costume at the shore.

"Always believe in your skills" Dadu enlightened me again.

Suddenly a sound came from our backside. It was somewhat familiar to that of the Robot.

It's time for level five. I was quite curious about that.

"Three parties are fighting here. Resolve anyone's fight."

 Next, we saw two Sumos wrestling with each other. Few yards ahead two deers & two cocks were fighting each other in the combo.

"It will fetch you to achieve your target easily" The Robotic voice echoed in our ears.

"Preventing a cock fight would be easier, should I opt for that?" I asked Dadu.

Dadu asked me to leave all the three parties at their fate & opted to move ahead.

"Why haven't you resolved the fight of any party, Dadu?" I asked him.

"Choose your battles wisely. Every battle is not worth winning. It was just another trap to waste our time.

See the hourglass! Only a few sand particles were left in the upper bulb. Our time is limited, as the sand in the upper bulb is getting lesser. If we stick to resolve the fight, we will lose our targets i.e., the aim to fetch a gold medal for you."

Next, we reached a big room full of glittering objects in bright yellow. It could be the gold coins that I presumed. I also noticed a heap of stones on the other side of the wall.

I sneaked out a gold coin into my pocket.

"You have reached the last level. Your prize is behind the wall, but you have to remove all the stones to get through the door near that wall. You can use this gold to pay the manpower that we would arrange for you. Then, a toss would be done with the coin that Ron had just sneaked out quietly in his pocket" The Robot again echoed from somewhere.

"How could they sense the coin in my pocket? " I complained to Dadu.

"CCTV cameras! My little thief!" Dadu said, pointing his finger towards one of them.

I understood the dynamics of the game fully by now.

"We would set aside the stones on our own" Dadu said after watching the trickling last sand particles from the upper bulb of the hourglass.

They were just the stones made of paper creating an illusion of something bulky. We set aside all of them with ease.

"Now, please toss the coin. If head comes, you will be eligible to take your prize & the tail would get you exit from the game" The nasty Robotic voice echoed again.

"We would not toss the coin. We would love to have an exit gate than to win by chance" Dadu said in anger.

I got a little bit tensed. It seemed that the gold medal was drifting away from us.

The Robot popped up on our right side screen to congratulate us. "It was the last test from our side to test your integrity."

"You have won all the levels. Sir! You have proved that no one can achieve success without an able teacher. Ron! You have got the best teacher by your side. You can also have the coin" The Robotic sound echoed in our ears. The voice got a bit sweeter for the first time. Now the door got opened. The room displayed the prize.

Finally, I got the gold medal with a certificate. The head of the museum had taken a selfie with us to get it printed in the leading newspaper of the nation. I was in cloud nine. At the exit gate, the same guard smiled.

"We have got two pieces of gold. One the medal & another the coin" I proudly told Dadu.

"Ok! Just scratch the coin a bit," Dadu said.

It was just chocolate wrapped in a golden wafer.Dadu smiled at me & said "Fame and success favour to those who choose their own path and don't imitate others".

Next morning, we flew back to Dehradun. At the aerodrome, I took out the magnifying glass from my bag. I began to watch the tiny sand particles of the hourglass carefully through it. The sand particles were receding to the lower bulb from the upper one.

"Our time is limited. I have to carve my own destiny". I said to myself. Those receding sand particles looked like the moments of my life spent in vain. "Time has come to spend each moment; aimed towards success & goals of my life, "I thought for a while & hugged Dadu for the greatest lessons of the life.

3. The secret of Robber's cave

Guys, it was just a lazy Sunday. To be precise, I have a special privilege on this auspicious day of the week.

I have the freedom of either watching my favourite shows on the television or playing any video game of my choice for the whole evening.

In addition; on this weekend my beloved parents had offered me a special bonanza- they were away from home for two day's business tour. It's always been a dream to be home alone.

My parents gave me some heavy doses of instructions regarding the Do's & Don'ts of maintaining discipline at the house yesterday. My mother even bribed me heavily for some chocolates after her return, if I would behave properly at par with her set standards.

It meant that everything should be at the designated place; the home should not look a mess on her arrival etc.

In the end, I got a strict lecture of my father regarding the same which I took more as a warning rather than a lesson.

According to me, every parent should take one or two days off from parenting to let all of their kids to manage the house.

I pounced upon the sofa like a crouching tiger to play my favourite video game. In the meantime, like a proud owner of this lavish home I even ordered my favourite pizza & cold drinks from a nearby outlet.

I played a video game for an hour. It was very strange that even my favourite pastime looked so boring, as nobody had yet disturbed me.It was the usual practice that I had to listen to mom's advice or father's scolding in between the gaming sessions.

It was regarding the waste of precious time while playing video games. But, it adds another spice & thrill to the gaming sessions.

The seasoning of spice was missing from the recipe. I assumed it as one of the prime reason for my boredom. My parents scolding between the gaming sessions add an extra flavour. I added it to my mind's learning curve.

So, I decided to switch my leisure activity to something more interesting.

I went to bed & covered myself fully inside the blanket except the eyes to watch a television show. I checked all the channels one by one - cartoon network, pogo etc.

Suddenly, an idea struck my mind. I must inculcate some attributes of a young boy. My parents always used to instruct me to shed off the mask of a kid & to become a responsible young lad. Even Dadu had advised me for that.

So, I decided to throw away the mask of childhood. As a kid, you are always expected to listen to everyone without raising a doubt. It was such a boring stuff. Now, the time has come to stretch your timeline to be at the younger side. The idea of having a girlfriend had started to knock my dreams every night.

It was time to enjoy the fantasies of a teenager.

So, I decided to watch horror show. It was 6 o'clock, the usual time of a pleasant sunset at Dehradun city. A captivating beginning of the show aroused my interest to carry on with it.

A man had turned into a ghost & he kept killing people on the highway.

He continued stopping a car as per his whims & fancies. He was killing everyone inside the vehicle through his axe. Then, that man entered into a cave having numerous skeletons lying sideways..........

Good heavens!

A sense of fear gripped me. All of a sudden, I began to perspire profusely out of nervousness.

My whole body was shivering.

Just then, the door of my room got opened by itself.

This was the last thing that I could resist. It was the time that I couldn't sustain anymore inside the room

I didn't even dare to watch the door side. Within a minute, I jumped right through the window that opened next to my Dadu's room.

It was a prompt decision to save myself from any possible impending disaster. At that moment, the younger boy in nebulous form inside me had disappeared and the same kid inside me was reborn.

I knocked Dadu's room very hard, hoping to have a glimpse of him. He was about to arrive that day after a scheduled tour from New Delhi.

My limbs were shivering with utmost fear. How could I dare to watch a horror show being home alone "What a fool am I?"I thought a bit & cursed myself.

Meanwhile, Dadu opened the door. I felt relieved & hugged him tightly. He nestled me on the sofa & enquired about the matter.

"So what brings you here in such haste & didn't you notice my arrival?" He asked me.

"Someone opened the door of my room. It could be a ghost" I yelled. My limbs were still shivering. I forgot his second question to answer out of fear.

"Ok! Let's go & inspect your room" He was still calm as if nothing had happened. I wondered a little.

We entered the room. My confidence level had risen in Dadu's company.

"Dadu is my saviour", my inner voice thanked me a bit & yielded a spy. We glanced at the room like a detective for some time.

"Ron! There was no one in the room. It must be wind" He replied me in a high pitched voice.

The horror show was still continuing on the television. It was enough for Dadu to analyse the situation. He even noticed the half-eaten pizza & the cold drink bottle lying on the table that I had ordered some time ago.

"So, my coward son! I got the whole issue. You were having a gala time. Also, it seemed that you were partying without inviting me!" Dadu probed me with a smile.

I got a bit embarrassed. "You are a diet conscious chap. So, I didn't invite you". I told him.

He made me rest on the bed. He paused for some time & started talking to me with a smile on his face.

"It was not your fault, Son! It's just a sign of bad parenting" A streak of happiness gleamed onto my face. "Now, Dadu would scold my parents, when they arrive from the tour. Then, they would understand my feelings "I imagined.

"OH! God! Please arrange that scolding sequence only in my presence "I prayed to God.

"Parents usually use fear as a tool to control their mischievous kids," Dadu said. His face turned into a philosopher mode.

"Yes! My mother used to frighten me every now & then; so that I could resist playing late in the evenings. She used to say that some sort of ghost would come right through the bushes to take me away with him."I explained to Dadu in a complaining tone. It will kindle Dadu's anger towards my parents more. I thought for a while.

Dadu gave a perched smile on my explanation.

"Hmmm! Even my mother did the same to me during my childhood. She always used to frighten me that some anonymous Baba(unscrupulous sage) would come & take me away" Dadu said to me.

"Did the Baba ever come to you?"I asked him.

"No! I am still waiting for him that one day he might come & have a welcome chat with me" Dadu replied me.

"Ah! So, we are victims of the same boat, Dadu" I said in surprise.

"Yes! Some sort of that" He replied again.

"Ron! Fear is a disability of the human mind. One has to tame that Frankenstein monster" He added further.

"Would you dare to come with me to beat that monster right now?"

It was another set of surprise by Dadu. I always consider him as a man with bundle of surprises.

"But! It's getting late in the night; 9 'clock to be exact" I informed him gazing at the watch.

"No, Dear! We will have a short trip to Robber's cave right now." He said.

I cursed that time when I decided to jump off the window and approached him for help. I must have covered myself in the blanket & let the Ghost do whatever he wanted to do with me. My conscience revealed to me.

I had been to Robber's cave once in my lifetime, on the school's picnic trip. It was a nice picnic spot. But to visit there, at night would be a nightmare for me.

It is some sort of a cave formed by two rocks with water flowing downstream.

I have heard many stories of misadventures near the highway connecting the cave.

But, Dadu kidnapped me into his jeep. I have used the word 'kidnapped' because the trip was about to happen against my will. Sheer contravention of child's rights.   But, who cares! I thought for a while.

It was a clear night. Orion constellation had just moved to a bit right as per my calculations. Meanwhile, He parked the car at one side of the highway after driving for half an hour.

We have to walk from here. Passage to robber's cave is through this forest. Around two km walk through the forest would reach us there". He told me like a curious guide, eager to keep their tourists at danger to showcase his skills & knowledge; even at haunted or banned places of tourist attraction.

Now, that Frankenstein monster named fear had gripped me more tightly. I remembered my parents. "Why did they leave me?" I thought for a while.

I held Dadu's hand more tightly. Dadu's presence or absence is not a matter of significance now.

 I started to compare him to that serial killer in the horror show, with himself leading me towards the cave full of skeletons.

A vague question came to my mind. "Is he really my Dadu or not? Had that serial killer transformed himself into the ghost that entered my room? Or had it transformed itself into my Dadu later on?"

We walked a hundred meters or so. All of a sudden, Something from the bushes alongside the road came in front of us. I hugged Dadu even more tightly.

"It's a porcupine, dear! It just popped up due to our torch beam" He said.

Dadu howled at him vigorously & it ran away from us. It helped me rebuild some courage within me.

Dadu gave me another lesson - "Everything has logic in life. No ghosts exist in real life. It is just a miss-conception."

We covered half the distance. Suddenly some bushes started to wave to my left side.

I watched Dadu's calm face, impatiently.

He gave me a bamboo stick & said to me in a loud tone "Ron! Go & overcome your fear".

With a heavy heart, I went close to the bushes & hopped that bamboo stick many times. It seemed as if I was beating that Frankenstein monster that was nicknamed as fear inside my conscience.

"No one is there in the bushes. It might be the gusty wind that had waved the bushes" I told Dadu.

"Great work, Ron! I am impressed" proud Dadu hailed my feat.

Now, we had reached the Robber's cave. An Owl had just hooted after seeing us. Its eyes were too vigilant & scary without any reason. I remembered the toppers of my class doing the same feat at night. My parents also nicknamed me as an owl. I didn't find any resemblance of myself, after watching it.

We entered the cave. Knee deep cold water going against the tide welcomed us.

We heard a peculiar sound. I gazed at Dadu's face for some hint.

He alluded me to keep quiet by pointing his finger at his mouth with a long...Shhhhhh!!!

Suddenly a group of bats passed over us. "They might have got disturbed by our presence" Dadu added. Don't worry & move ahead.

The monster of fear had diminished very much from my side. It's like that when you switch bathing from warm to cold water; you feel jittery at first, but after some time you enjoy it.

"Shall we go now? " I asked him.

"Not yet! A surprise is awaiting you". Dadu said.

Dadu took me to a place where the stream ends. From there, we passed through a lean passage.

"Oh, wow! "I screamed with joy.

The place was somewhat like a fairyland. It was nearly an enclosed space with a pond at the centre. Fireflies were flying all around, creating an illusion of twinkling stars at night. The water in the pond was bright blue; being illuminated by bioluminescent Dinoflagellates. Small fishes of every colour were inside the pond. That place was just like another heaven.

"How do you come to know about this place, Dadu?"I enquired.

"No one dared to come here at night due to false fables that created confusion & fear in the local's mind. Only I had overcome that fear & thus got the surprise". He told me.

I praised Dadu for his fearless adventure skills.

We rested there for three hours. Meanwhile, I swam across the pond. I found some glittery objects at the bottom. OH! To my surprise, I found oysters. I picked up four of them & even extracted two pearls. It was nearly 4 o'clock. "Time to leave for home" Dadu told me.

At the exit of that cave, an animal's shadow fell to our side. At once, I took the bamboo stick from Dadu and ran to search it. It was a deer. I assumed myself as Mowgli and chased him to some distance. Frankenstein monster called 'fear' had left my soul by now. The deer ran as fast as he could.

I joined Dadu again. He praised my courage.

"After we overcome our greatest fears, the far greater and sweet become the fruits of success. In addition, don't forget to apply logic in every aspect of your life. A gentleman without logic is similar to a fool." He said.

"You may call me an urban Mowgli now for sure," I told him proudly.

"A brave one! "He added & smiled again.

We headed towards the highway. After some time, Dadu drove me away to the home. In the meantime, I took out the magnifying glass & a cubical showpiece that was lying on the deck of the jeep. Some coloured thermo Cole balls were getting disturbed violently amidst the packed cube having a single outlet.

I moved the magnifying glass over it. It was a tiny insect struggling to get past the obstacle to get out of the hole and trying to overcome his fear with hope & logic. I helped it out.

4. Corporate student

Our school curriculum had a project to study about the 'corporate world'.

Every student had to write a compulsory project report about the office activities at their father's office.

The class teacher said that it would help us to carve a professional outlook.

For a few days, I pretended to be an ideal son, although my father knew me very well. I was trying to ease the troubled relationship between us.

One week had passed, I wore a veil of an ideal son that my heart wanted to throw off as early as possible. I had not committed any mistake in that period. Neither any complaint message had come from school into my father's cell phone inbox.

Even none of my neighbours had approached him with my complaint that may cause any bad reputation to his name. It was a record. My mom would love to get my name registered into the Guinness book of records.

I had deputed my mother as a mediator. She had already informed about the report making project to my father. He was a chief executive head at a reputed sales firm.

He was promoted from a chartered accountant to Chief executive head in just eight years in his company. My Dadu used to tell me proudly about his son's success story.

Next day, I woke up early with my Dadu. I intimated him about my plans of visiting father's office today. He told me that he would drop me two hours earlier at my father's office.

I entered the Dehradun business centre; Floor no. 5. The nameplate read "Doon Associates."

The guard was still asleep inside the lift. It must be his night shift. It had eased my entry into the office. I reached two hours earlier than the usual office time. The officials at the night shift duty had logged out of the system. They were waiting to leave the office near a biometric attendance machine.

"Is this the office of Mr Alter?" I asked an official.

He nodded into 'yes'.

"What made you come here? I have not seen any kids coming to this office so far". He enquired to me.

"I am a new recruit to this office. People call me as a child prodigy. I completed my Masters in commerce at the age of twelve itself" I tried to prank him.

"Mr Alter was very much impressed with my skills. He had recruited me at this office. It was my first day here". I continued.

Well, it worked. He was impressed with me.

"Welcome to the office!" He said & left the venue after punching his attendance.

I entered the office. No one noticed me. The display board at the entrance had informed me that Neha, the personal assistant will be on leave today. I sat at her designated cabin. I could see all the activities of the office floor area & my father's cabin from there. The office floor had three rows of cabinets arranged side by side. Evidently, I gave A-plus grade to the Interior Designer in my random thoughts.

At sharp 9:30 AM, my father arrived at the office premises.Everyone stood up to greet him. The protocols were similar to our school, except for the prayer sessions.

The boss from higher management came & banged the file on my father's table. I want results, Mr Alter. I could listen to the conversation in my father's cabin. I had already messaged him about my whereabouts in the office.

"Let your boys do some more hard work" The official was furious at him.

My father was in self-control mode. He remained calm & humble. His attitude was surprisingly opposite to that of home. I have seen a different father at his office, compared to our home.

"Okay, I would work at this project again" He peeked through the file & rounded some points quickly via a highlighter.

"You will find it finished within two days." He told him in a soft tone.

The official had left the office. My father called an executive from the office floor and said to him "The file that you have completed had returned. The boss was furious at me. What the hell they want from us? These people had made our work ethics like hell". He tossed the paperweight softly in the air.

 "You are asked to complete this file work again. I understand that you are a new recruit. But, try to hold the responsibilities on your shoulder.

Rework on this file. Please make sure that it should not come back to me from my superiors.

Do it as per the client's requirements. I had already highlighted some major issues in it" He told him without a pause.

 I thought that the new recruit would get a serious bashing from my father.

 But I was wrong.

My father called the new recruit again and advised him to feel free to ask him if he is stuck somewhere in work. I was awestruck at my father's politeness. If it would be me in the place of the new recruit, he would have slapped me until the work is done.

"When would the Vendor's client come?" He called up someone. "We have messaged him thrice. Even my patience has a limit. It's already an hour late" He said further. It seemed that he had applied the scent of politeness.

If it would be our home, our father would have ridiculed us. But, he is quiet now.

"It's a corporate meet, Sneha. Please arrange it in my cabin. I'm tired" He called up from the conference room.

There was an ultimate discipline in the office. It was a disciplined place with or without the boss. I recollected how we used to make a mess at our school when a teacher is absent in the class by shouting at each other.

The meeting was held to discuss strategies, to grab a project. Plan A & B were discussed. "Our school life is without plans." I thought for a while.

In the end, everybody gave a presentation to understand the market scenario.

The SWOT analysis was done. Responsibilities were assigned to every person. Everyone seemed loyal & passionate about their work that was assigned.

We even struggle to do homework & question our teachers, if the question paper came out of syllabus.

It was a way different place from our school life. "What made them so obedient, loyal & disciplined?" I wondered.

"You are late. What's wrong? Are you stuck somewhere? Ok leave it, let's start.

Please be seated, Mr Taneja. "My father accommodated another employee in between the meet.

I have seen him as a man of action, flexible enough to accommodate everyone. I was a way different from him, complaining over silly odds and even fighting over petty issues.

During the lunch break, "What motivates you to work so hard?" I asked him.

"Its family, Ron" He answered swiftly.

Every day is a day of exam & results, failure & joy at the office. All emotions come into play at this 1000 sq. Feet office floor - Happiness, rejection, hope & despair, etc., I felt it a way similar to our school.

Later, my father came to the office floor to announce something exciting.

"A new project was awarded to us. Hope we all will cooperate towards its success." All the employees clapped & expressed happiness with a wide range of emotions.

One hour was left to complete that day's office time.

To my surprise, a cake was kept ready. Everyone came to the office floor.

"We have two birthdays today. One of your beloved boss & the other one was of our beloved peon – Mr Gupta" He announced happily. He offered the peon to cut the cake. Mr Gupta looked a bit shy at that proposal.

Finally, both of them cut the cake. Everybody congratulated & wished them good luck. The peon was overwhelmed by the officers' gestures.

My father's report card of that day was-

More than 100 phone calls were attended. Twenty appointments were cleared.

Another ten were planned for the coming week. My one day's school task was his fifteen minutes share. So many issues were in the queue for him. But, who could he blame?

He kept his cool in every situation & overcame all problems with ease.

One thing that I came to know now is- "my father is a kind-hearted man as a whole"

Every child must visit their respective father's office to get to know how the parents work hard at the office for their children & family.

After the office, I sat next to my father for the first time in the car.

I panned the magnifying glass towards his face.

"Ron! When will you be matured?"

"I had learnt some lessons regarding it today, at your office. Even a lot about you."

I told him.

"What? About me?" He questioned.

"You are like a coconut shell. Harder outside and softer inside."

He smiled at me. I hugged him for the first time.

Hope the relation between us will grow and mature henceforth.

HOURGLASS
The Second Gift

The more sand has escaped from the hourglass of our life, the clearer we should see through it.

- Niccolo Machiavelli

5. World of Zombies

6. The time – machine

7. A wise Peculiar Rabbit

8. Love your Mom…Forgive your Father

5. World of Zombies

It was 31st October; the day of Halloween. Devil within us was about to unleash free. My friend's group had already decided on the theme - 'Zombie'. Our parents also gave us a free rein to pull pranks. Our agenda was to scare people that we disliked. Yesterday, we made a detailed list of this.

The first on the 'hit list' was Gupta Uncle, my next-door neighbour. He had never returned us any cricket ball; ever since we started playing gully cricket. A flighted cricket shot towards his home would mean the ball getting lost.

For a few years; we had tried to get the ball back but later on, we left the idea. We assumed it as a 'haunted home' for the cricket balls. Frequent loss of the balls compelled us to make a distinct rule.

A leg-side six destined towards his home was declared to be out, with a rupee fine. That fine would make up for buying another ball. It was against the cricket rule books, but a necessity for us.

Next on the list was our class teacher. A legally paid spy sincerely dedicated to the service of our parents. She never said anything good about us.

Parents-teacher's meet was her favourite day at school. Others were the soft targets. It was some of our classmates. Rest of them are the girls in our class, who didn't help in our assignments.

My father & principal were excluded due to the super-powers they had. One armed with the 'rustication' orders and the other being the economic powerhouse of the home.

As I woke up early in the morning; I started preparations for the Halloween party. At first, the dress up and next would be the makeup.

I got my old pair of casuals & spritz black tea including mud all over them to get a 'faded' zombie looking costume. I made my hair greasy with chocolate syrup to get a dirty look & even burnt the lower sides of my jeans.

Next, I smeared black food colouring on my tongue & tomato ketchup all over my clothes. Even, I put some tomato ketchup sachets in my pocket. It was to create an instant 'blood scene' to look real in front of our victims.

Now, I went to my mother's room to apply some makeup on my face. I used all the possible combinations of black & brown shades on my face & much darker at the eye sockets. The idea was to get a perfect 'zombie' look.

Now, the time had come to cross-check the effects of the Zombie look. My mom woke up. I approached her, walking & shuffling towards the bed. She yelled in fear for help.

It confirmed that my 'Zombie look' had scary characteristics. I asked her to stop screaming. If my father would have come to save her, then it would ruin my day.

"It was me, your son Ron! Dear Mom". I told her immediately.

"What the hell you have done to yourself?" - She replied in surprise.

"Just got ready for the Halloween party at school" I replied promptly.

"You look so scary! But, you don't need to adorn a zombie look. Your looks and mischief are pretty similar to Zombies without the make-up". She said with a smile & left to the kitchen.

It disturbed me a bit. "After all, it's my mom. Never mind!" I thought to myself and moved on.

I called up my friends to assemble at Gupta's mansion. It was the time when he opens his door for the milkman. Everyone knows that the time selection is very crucial in pulling the pranks.

I ringed the doorbell. My friends were behind me. We had already applied fresh tomato ketchup all over the body & lips; just then.

As soon as Mr Gupta opened the door, we formed a human chain & started shuffling with slight stumbling action in a synchronized way to look like a real 'Zombie' group. Fear had gripped Mr Gupta. He ran back to his bedroom and shut the door with a bang. It was quite a successful prank. We snatched most of our cricket balls from his drawing-room. He had made a show-piece wrapped in glittery polythene sheets of different colours with them.

Excited with our plan getting right, we headed towards the school in the same fashion. But, the plan was backfired! Five street dogs hounded us. The Zombie fever within us disappeared. We ran for a safe & appropriate shelter. "We looked like jokers to the dogs, maybe" I imagined.

Ron's Best Gifts ever – samar deep singh

We ran towards the fenced mound at the nearby park to save ourselves. We waited for some time & hired an auto-rickshaw to reach the school. We scared the fairy turned girls of our class at our school compound, later on. The first rule of the Halloween is that the zombies hated the fairies.

We approached our class teacher at the staff-room to scare her a bit.

"Nice dress up, boys! Now you have donned yourselves in real characters" - She said without a single streak of fear in her eyes.

"Because, you are really like zombies in your studies" - she added further.

Her face showed no emotions altogether. To our surprise, she even threatened us for the upcoming Halloween party.

She hinted that she would dress up into scarier outfit than that of ours.

"Dear Miss! You are scaring us every day since we had been admitted to the school. You don't need another outfit for that" I said to myself.

It was a perfect evening at Dehradun. Now, the Halloween party had started at the school auditorium. We danced & pulled pranks with each other. We have taken a lot of selfies & enjoyed the gala time. The whole class photograph was taken at last.

Our class teacher had donned a 'fox' theme. She looked like that. Her costume matched the character as well.

I came home after the Halloween party & went straight to Dadu's room. I gestured a zombie look at him, but he stood calm & blank.

"Do we have zombies in real life?" I asked him.

He nodded into a big 'Yes' and hinted me to get a decent bath first.

I came to his room after a short while & sat at the sofa with a pillow in my hands, a perfect posture to listen to a story.

"Yes, my son!" He replied after a short pause. He elaborated his answer to my question further hence:

I have seen the zombies all around the town. My father was posted at Meerut. The news at the All India Radio tensed the coming 'Holi' festival fervour. Communal riots 'broke' out in the city. I was around twelve years old at that time. Just, as you are right now. But, I was naughtier and impulsive than you.

We were returning from school one day, after participating in a fancy dress competition. It was very late in the evening. I had donned into a clown. My friend Rashid had donned into a typical 'Gandhi' attire.

There was an uneasy silence on the streets.

Our parents were eagerly waiting for us.

They rushed us into our respective home with an unexplained hustle.

I could sense the fear in their eyes.

We dwelled at a rented home. Mr Khan was my father's best friend & our landlord too. Rashid was Mr Khan's only son & my classmate too. Mr Khan locked all five of us, including my grandparents & parents in a room on the first storey, to ensure our safety.

Two days had passed. We hid there with limited food & water. I asked my father about the situation multiple times, but he never responded. His eyes showed impending fear & concern of bleak future.

The room had a 'worn out' door with a wide-open crack at its bottom left side. From that crack, the fine street view was evident.

Next day, a streak of sunlight fell through the crack to get us aware of another morning. I came close to that crack to watch the street as a pastime measure.

The street was all 'Red' with the blood. People were running haphazardly in groups, armed with knives, swords, hockey sticks etc. All of a sudden, the two groups came close & started to quarrel with each other. Around ten people were lying unconscious on the streets with the blood all around.

Expressions of fear were evident on my face. My mother sensed it. She kept me away from the door. Now, I understood the whole scenario.

An impulsive & naughty child had turned into a mature one within a few minutes. An uneasy silence & fear gripped the whole family. Only Rashid was allowed to enter the room in the afternoon from the back door.

I had an idea. We wanted to divert our parents' attention. I wore a clown dress & began cutting some sharp jokes. Looking at me, Rashid also wore his Gandhi attire. He gave a short speech after my performance, stating-

"An eye to eye makes the whole world blind........"

After a long time, my parents had a little smile on their faces. With the first ray of the sun approaching the door's crack the next day, I went there & watched the street scene.

It was really like Zombies walking & hurting each other without a cause. "Ah! The communal zombies, to be precise" Dadu emphasized the word thrice.

The food was getting lesser with each passing day. My parents had their meals only once a day by now.

One day, a hard knock was heard at the door that blocked the incoming sunlight completely & our hopes too. No sun rays approached through the door's hole.

It must be the afternoon. My whole family was silent & full of fear throughout that time.It was Rashid standing with a hoe in his right hand. His father carried the sword to defend us from the mob.

"There is nobody inside," He told the mob.

He prayed to them to get away from their house. My parents got a bit tensed.Rashid blocked the wide-open crack. Suddenly, a frenzied party on the streets diverted their attention. They moved to the streets again.

My mother didn't allow me to watch the scene on the street. I watched the hourglass kept at the cupboard. The sand particles were trickling from upper to the lower bulb. It was given by my father to keep track of the time. "You are losing your precious time like the sand dripping from the upper to lower bulb"- He said that quite often.

I prayed to God to get them to trickle faster.

My grandfather gazed the street from the wide-open crack "For this day, we had fought the freedom struggle" - He added further, with tears in his eyes and continued.

Peace had turned into violence; harmony to jealousy; hope to despair & love had faded into hate. Women & children were the worst affected by the riots in the town.

Dadu concluded with another short pause. People assembled into groups to rob and kill each other. They all looked like the zombies hurting each other and spreading the virus of 'hate' and 'negative thoughts'. They were the victims of negativity.

"They were truly the real-life zombies, Dadu!" I told him.

"Yes! People who spread communal violence are the zombies in reality" He told me.

"So, how did you manage to survive?" I asked him impatiently.

It was the fifteenth day of our confinement in that tiny room. The siren of the paramilitary forces hooted in the evening. My father saw a flag march done by the security forces through the crack. It kindled hope & confidence in his eyes.In the evening, Mr Khan opened the door. "The law and order situation is under control now," He said with a smile on his face.

"But the town is still under curfew" He added further.We had a sigh of relief.Mr Khan quoted favourite lines of Mahatma Gandhi – "Ishwar Allah tero naam sabko sanmati de bhagwaan".

"The zombie episode had ended in the town. The peace & harmony had returned in the meantime" Dadu concluded.I was quite silent. I could understand Dadu's sentiments at that tough time. After a while, I slept into Dadu's arms watching the trickling sand of the hourglass silently. "We should face the tough time with grit & bravery"- was my thought for that night.

6. The Time-machine

My

grandfather had a knack of getting mysterious at times. He usually talks about the picturesque beauty & awe-inspiring landscapes of the Ladakh valley.

The rough & rugged mountainous terrain had numerous unsolved mysteries, yet to be resolved. The valley had scintillating snow-covered peaks and streams that flow through the deep valleys, but it was sparsely populated.

He had hinted me about the strange stories of UFO's (Unidentified Flying Objects) landing at night. He told me about the mysterious fables crafted by the local residents. But, he had never admitted about any government-sponsored scientific or technical research undergoing there. He never accepted the UFO stories as real. Every time, I dared to search the secrets deeper, he felt a bit tensed & uncomfortable.

One night, he was sneaking out from the house. He took out his jeep parked inside the garage. I was aware of his activities as he slept earlier without talking to me last night. It had invoked a spy within me. Multiple spy stories rocked my mind.

Had he got a girlfriend or a wife with another family, to whom he was heading to meet them secretly? If I could decipher that, the friendly reunion with my father could be possible then.

I hid at the back seat of the jeep quietly. He didn't notice me. He was driving furiously. Either his girlfriend must have been kidnapped or his wife had been pregnant waiting to seek immediate attention. Another coherent sequence of thoughts rocked my mind.

The All India radio had predicted the heavy snowfall in the Himalayan region of India in the next few days. As a caution, the Manali-Leh route had to be closed for a few days. He was desperate to reach the destined place as early as possible.

In the morning, a stunning panoramic view of sunrise awakened me. But the extreme weather took a heavy toll on my health. I contracted cold & cough. I was panting heavily. Heavy episodes of sneezing made Dadu recognize me. He stopped the jeep.

"Ron! What are you doing here? I have told you not to accompany me". He asked me in a harsh tone.

"I am sorry, Dadu. I was worried about you". I told him.

Suddenly, the All India Radio had popped up a bulletin again. All the highways up to Dehradun had been closed due to heavy snowfall.

Now, he was in a fix. He couldn't go back. I was happy that I could have the opportunity to unravel some of his secrets.

I sat at the front seat like a boss. He wrapped a blanket around me.

I was quite for around two hours. He gazed at me as if I had ruined his honeymoon plans or so.

"You are without questions today!" He said in surprise as if I was an unwanted guest that he had to entertain, under an obligation.

"I thought that we don't have any unfamiliar secrets with us. I have shared all my secrets with you. Even, about my crush Sonia". I got a bit emotional. I tried to pop up a few tears too.

He smiled a bit. The relation between us was about to break some ice.

His face had turned into the same philosophical mode. Maybe the weather prediction was not good. But I had cleared the weather of doubt between us to some extent. The mist of tensed relations between us had already been cleared by now.

He paused for a minute.

"Some secrets must be buried and not meant to be revealed to anyone". He replied in a soft tone.

"I thought that we were good friends and that there is no room for the secrets between us, as you also had said once" I replied him emotionally with a few false tears again. An unmatched formula to quench the rest of anger left at his heart.

He smiled a bit. I felt quite relaxed. I have got the same Dadu.

The weather had got quite more abnormal apart from the usual temperature close to the freezing point. Only a dedicated lover could have summoned that courage to beat that harsh weather.

My spy theories about Dadu's girlfriend had got some more flesh. "Will Dadu's another family welcome me or not". I thought a bit.

Such strange ideas kept me busy throughout the journey.

"Some secrets are like an addiction, and they should be kept within us. You have not gained that age to get yourself familiar about all of this". He said after a significant pause.

I was quite actively engaged in listening to his philosophical part, that I was unaware of. "Come on, Dadu! Please get a bit more emotional and reveal the name of your girlfriend or wife". My heart started beating heavily.

Until now, I have seen my class teacher getting into this mode. She gets quite emotional about the future of students who didn't study. The toppers at the front benches used to supply her tissue papers to let her sob properly.

It was confirmed that it would not be an ordinary secret. It's got to be somewhat more secretive & exciting. On the whole, we have finished one day of the ride. We halted many times to have the local refreshment.

Meanwhile, he had also messaged my parents about my whereabouts.

We reached a deserted place. It was evening. The beauty of Ladakh was at its best. The snow-clad Zaskar range made the sunset mesmerizing to watch.

We halted at the helipad. It had led us to a tunnel that gave space to a large military facility.

A fat guard at the entrance didn't like my presence. "Sir! You knew that we don't allow kids at the premises" He said to Dadu quite softly.

"No, I have grown up a lot. I had cleared seven classes with distinction in drawing & arts". I intervened.

The guard got puzzled for a while, but he was not at all impressed by me.

Dadu told me to keep quiet.

"I will talk to the Programme Director, please let him in". He told the guard.

"I have no option to get him back to his home due to bad weather. I assure you that he will behave properly and all the information will remain classified" He assured the guard patting him softly at his back.

"But, we have to tie a black cloth around his eyes so that he could not see our premises". He said.

"I said a big 'yes' to them. A Bollywood style welcome of a hero" I felt a bit.

"Go ahead!" Dadu replied to the guard.

It was a unique place having different sounds that came from every corner of the premises.

"What's this facility is all about?" I asked Dadu to silence my curious spy mind.

It's some sort of a launch pad facility for rockets. Assume that the rockets were being deployed to the outer world from here. I am still not getting the picture clearer. He was still talking to me like a layman.

But, with such a secretive way; the premises was under doubt.

We halted for some time, at a small cabin. He opened my cloth tied around my eyes.

"What are we waiting for?" I asked him impatiently.

"They are preparing a machine" he replied.

"For which reason? Will they launch us to Mars?" I asked him again.

"It's some sort of a time machine" He replied.

"Will it take us to our future?" I asked him with curiosity.

"It does not take us to the future. It will lead us to our past." He replied to me.

"Dadu! Why can't we sense future through this machine? I wanna see my future girlfriend" I told him.

"We are having a bit of research on this issue too. We will inform you one day if we succeed" He told me in anger and looked a bit irritated this time.

"Why we only see past through this" I questioned him again.

"People tend to reconcile easily with their past, be it good or bad," He said with a smile on his face.

"Sorry! I don't understand" I told him instantly.

"With which are you more concerned with- The past report cards with their marks or the upcoming one of this year? " Dadu tried to clear my doubt.

"Yes! Indeed, the upcoming one, I have forgotten the past ones and don't even care for them" I answered him. His example satisfied me.

"Listen! Since we are in the same machine. We can see each other's past too. We are both connected. We can feel each other's life memories".

"Can we use it to find secrets of any enemy or spy?" I asked him, forgetting that the machine cannot predict the future.

"Yes! You are getting smarter with each passing day" He replied.

I smiled a bit. I was really excited about all that.

"Now, Please be silent and don't talk; just experience". He said.

Suddenly, I felt numb. The mind penetrated the memories that even I was not aware of. Some memories are lost from our subconscious mind. But they are always present within our conscience. It was a great feeling! Like picking up a photo album and watching the pictures per se.

A streak of light entered my mother's womb; I found the heartbeat and myself too. When she touched her stomach; my heartbeat got connected with her. I loved the sensation when she touched her belly.

 She kept talking to me every now & then. Her voice made me happy and content.

The world is different outside. I will teach you how to deal with it safely. She used to tell me frequently.

Whenever she talked to me, I gave her bump a jerk. My hands were not yet developed, so I gave her a kick as a sign of thumbs up.

"See! The baby listens to me more than you. We will have a dearest bond" She told my father.

It was the large football ground, and the match was in progress.

"Darling, It was the goal" father shouted in excitement.

I also kicked multiple times on my mother's bump.

"See! Your baby is also having goals at the bump. Just feel it."

"Yes! He will play football someday for sure" My father told her.

Nothing could be ever pious and honoured than the mother's struggle to introduce a baby to this world. It is the purest sign of love, sacrifice & devotion.

We also tried it hard and succeeded. "Sorry for the labour pain, mom."

The world was not yet sweet. It was the same hospital and the room of my house thereafter.

Once, my mother and I went out of the house on the baby stroller pram. I started connecting with the beauty of this world. My first outing to the park and the shopping mall was awesome.

Everybody was watching and smiling at me. I felt like a celebrity. I wished if I had strong hands, then they would surely get my autographs.

Every girl and aunt used to kiss my cheeks and shower love to me. But, the stardom had got lost with my increasing age.

The first steps to learn walking and lessons of my mother were quite handy. She picked me up every time and encouraged me without fail. Amazingly, I found my father very excited and he too helped me every time.

I wonder why we forget our parent's struggle in getting us to grow up. If anyone gets to know about this, through this time machine; the strained relations of old aged parents with their young son or daughter would certainly get healed up.

I hated when the elders touched my cheeks. I had given all the rights of touching and kissing; only to my beloved mother.

I failed to recognize my father in a beard. My mother always scolded him to be clean shaved in front of the baby.

It seemed like spinning against gravity and watching my life events in real; in the time machine.

On the other side, I found my grandfather in tears. He was sobbing.

I saw a handsome young man at front row watching the beauty pageant. A beautiful woman in a miss world costume slipped accidentally into his arms.

"Thanks for saving me" she replied softly, handling the miss world tag wrapped around her dress.

"Can you leave me now? I have to give some autographs" She told the young man with a smile. He was my Dadu at his young age.

"Sorry! I can't; unless you give the first one to your saviour" He replied her.

She blushed a bit and did the same afterwards.

He followed her everywhere, she went. Both had a common friend - a tarot card reader. Another meeting was arranged by the common friend between the two that had become quite successful.

It was the most difficult night for him. He was drafting a love letter for her love interest. The dustbin had got filled with the waste papers due to the multiple failed attempts. After many such attempts, he got success.

He went to Dresden square. She opened the gate. He gave the letter to her, wrapped in a red rose.

She opened the letter. The lady shouted in anger. How dare you come here like this!?

After a minute of silence, she yelled at the young man.

"I thought that you would propose me in a much more exciting way". She said.

"Dear, I am also desperate to marry you. I love you so much and can't live without you" She hugged him. The first kiss followed thereafter. He proposed her at once.

 "It was the only thing that Dadu had done at the right time," I thought for a while.

The engagement rings were exchanged after a few days at a grand ceremony. He could feel it now. He was rubbing his finger.

After a few weeks, both got married.

An unfateful car accident had separated the couple. I saw him sobbing outside the operation theatre for the loss. His eyes were closed. He couldn't watch that sequence. I held his hand tightly. We decided to stop the machine.

Dadu pressed the return switch.

 "You loved your wife that much?" I asked him.

"Just one sight of her gave me the hope to live life at its best. It was like an addiction, ever since I had opted as a volunteer here;   to test this machine" He told me emotionally.

"Listen! We were a part of the experiment and our experiences . had got recorded as well. Please do not reveal it to anyone" Dadu advised me further.

"Why there were no records of yours after my birth" I enquired him.

He said sorry for this as he was busy in that 'time machine' project.

Both of us set out for Dehradun.

I watched the trickling sand of the hourglass at the car deck. In those tiny particles, our sweetest memories were being recorded into the sands of time.

7. A wise Peculiar Rabbit

The school bus services were stopped en route school due to lesser number of students and long distance from the bus stop, adjacent to my home. My parents had arranged a mini school van for us. Only four students commuted through it.

Both the journey and the van driver were quite boring.

Another headache was his tuned old emotional Bollywood songs from the van stereo. In addition, he used to sing those songs in his hoarse voice; which exceeded the limits, we could tolerate.

The frequent breakdown of the van during the journey would lead us to push it to a few meters, alongside the highway. Our repeated complaints on our hardships were neither heard by the parents, nor by the van driver. Sometimes, he repeats his failed love story, for which we are bound to appreciate him too.

An idea crept into one of our minds. If we could harass the van driver then we could get rid of him, with a bonus of school holidays; until our parents find another alternative.

A conspiracy to get rid of him was made ready. We changed the school dress to formals and sat in the van for our usual journey to home. He enquired for the odd dress change, but we made an excuse saying that we got bored wearing the school dress; all day long. He smiled and did not get any clue about our plans. As we reached the highway, we started to shout violently.

"Help us! The van driver is kidnapping us". We all shouted at once.

One of us went an extra mile & added -" to make us beg. Listen to us! The future of our nation is in danger".

A police patrol vehicle ran after the van. The driver got a bit confused. He made another mistake that fuelled our innocence to the police. He increased the speed of the van after noticing the police.

After ten minutes of chase, the police had succeeded in catching the driver. He was immediately arrested. Though, the driver was explaining to the police that he was our school van driver, deputed by our parents and not a kidnapper. The police couldn't get convinced by him.

We thanked the officers for helping us. But, to escape from them was quite challenging. However, we managed to skid from their suspicious minds. Finally, they retrieved our addresses and sent us safely to our respective home, with police escort.

To my bad luck, it was late in the evening; by the time I reached home. Everyone was at home. The police officials took our statement and told my father to cross sign the FIR application.

My father was furious at me. He was waiting for the police officials to depart.

He told the officials that it was the children's gimmick. He also explained to them that he knew the bus driver and he was an honest man.

The officials warned us and left home.

What had happened to me and how nicely I was punished thereafter; I would not like to divulge it here. Else, it would fetch another child rights violation case against my parents.

The spiral of punishments would always continue. It would be better to embrace the punishment rather than to continue the spiral.

After all of this had ended, I came to my Dadu's room seeking some comfort and insisted upon him to tell a story. Dadu started to narrate that one.

There was a family of rabbits residing in a village. The spring had approached with sprawling meadows all over the landscape.

The ground had turned into a lush green carpet. The happiness was around the corner as the twins were born in that family.

One of them was so peculiar that everyone from nearby villages came to visit him. He had a shining round clock attached to his chest. At the periphery of the clock, six beautiful stones were embedded around it. That peculiar baby rabbit had become a buzz around the village. Even the king visited him and showered blessings with luxurious gifts. Irrespective of age, everybody was talking about him; wondering whether the peculiar rabbit would be a sign of good luck or just an omen of some curse.

Meanwhile, her mother was pleased with the siblings and more proud of his peculiar baby.

One night, the room was lit with a streak of dim light followed by a strange but pleasant sound. Mother lit the torch in surprise.

Good heavens!

It was the peculiar baby rabbit born with a golden clock, round in shape and firmly attached to his chest. The surprise had ended within five minutes. The clock also started ticking. The mother found it very unusual but, she nestled the baby rabbit to her chest.

Everything happens for a reason. "Jesus! Please help us". She murmured after making a cross sign over the baby's forehead. She slept after a while but, the baby rabbit was still awake.

His parents loved him very much. He always gave a confused look to everyone around him, but he had a calm & subtle behaviour. His actions always showed the patience of a sage.

The clock attached to the rabbit had some other strange markings too. It had stones of different colours embedded around the clock's periphery. One of them had just turned white to blue that night.

The baby rabbit knew the secret behind it, which has marked his birth. It meant that his time had started on this earth.

 Some mysteries are yet to be unfolded about that clock, by him too.

The days had passed by and had spun into years. He showered immense love on his parents. He was a darling to his father as he knew that the time left with his father was very less.

On an unlucky day, he was playing outside his home. The clock had lit bright with a pleasant humming sound. Suddenly, he ran to his house and enquired about his father's whereabouts.

His mother told him in a depressed voice that his father had turned into a star at the sky and would only be visible at night. His surprise had turned into extreme grief of his life.

He came to know that those studded bright stones embedded in the clock were linked to a special event at his life; quite special & definite.

One hand of the clock had spun the area of fifteen degrees already. He concluded that the rest of the unswept area implied the course of his life.

The clock had shown that fifteen per cent of it was spent and the rest was left behind. That episode had enlightened him enough about the embedded stones at the clock's periphery & his life.

After a year, another stone had gleamed bright & turned blue. It was her mother's favourite stone embedded inside the clock. Earlier one that was lit was his father's favourite.

He screamed with grief! It was my mother's favourite stone. He thought for a while.

He came to his home and told his bedridden mother about it in a depressed tone.

His mother held his hand and said - "I knew it. It started gleaming, but I was very fortunate to have you in my life. You have taken care of mine so well". She paused for a minute.

"It's ok, my son. I would be quite happy to become a star in the sky adjacent to your father.

You made me happy and proud throughout my life". His mother told him further. That night, she left both the siblings.

The wise peculiar rabbit hugged his brother and cried his heart out.

"Every incident of destruction done by God has a silver lining. Everything happens for a reason & with a strict timeline, so never curse the Almighty". He incited some words of wisdom to his brother.

Since then, everyone he met in his life, he showered love & affection. The perfect state of nirvana and bliss was attained. The clock had taught him the art of living and the meaning of life. He knew that everyone's time is limited.

So, one has to use it wisely. A prompt gaze to clock's hand assured him of the bitter truth.

"The rabbit grew into a teen. It was those youthful days that most of us spend without doing anything productive and which direct our nice future". Dadu said to me.

But the rabbit was intelligent enough. Both the brothers had found a decent job. He never confronted his brother & showered an intense love and affection with fatherly guidance every time.

The job was quite boring, but he stuck to that. He had to unload a bucket of carrots from the fields to the farmhouse. In return, the boss never offered him carrots to eat as a token, but only some rupees as wages.

I interrupted Dadu saying, "So mean was the boss! Dadu. Rabbits love carrots".

"That's the situation exactly similar to my mother's job". I added further.

Dadu asked me to prove it.

"She works at the bank as a cashier. She has bundles of rupee notes, but her boss never gave any".

Dadu smiled a little & nodded into a big 'yes'. He paused for some time and continued the story again.

One day, on the way to his job; he saw a pretty hare doing some household odds. Since then, he had made a routine to see her. He sets out earlier for the job just to have a glimpse of her.

Once, our hero the peculiar rabbit dared to ask her name.

She told him in a sweet voice – "Harley, my dear!". She blushed and hid inside the home, which was a beautiful burrow along the main street.

"Love at the first sight!" I added. At which, Dadu smiled a bit.

With time, both had become best friends.

One of the stones of the clock gleamed bright & turned blue. For the first time, it had brought happiness in his life.

He concluded that the embedded stones in the clock don't resemble any good or bad luck in his life. They are just the events.

It was on the 14th of February. To the world, it was Valentine's Day. To our hero peculiar rabbit, it was the day of do or die. He had to propose the hare today.

He went to her home. She was all alone, waiting for him.

He entered the home and gifted a bottle of champagne along with a bouquet of roses to her. Next, he offered a ring to her and proposed in a romantic tone.

"Will you marry me!? My dear Harley!"

She said "Yes!"   And the stone gleamed bright with a noticeable sound. Both had got married very soon.

In due course of time, he was blessed with two children. But, the clock hand had traversed sixty per cent. He knew that he would not be able to get with them throughout his life.

He nurtured them with immense love and care, cherishing every moment of their childhood. The children grew younger and kept busy in their job & family.

On one unfateful night, the stone that his wife loved had turned bright and turned to blue. She too turned into stars at the sky.

Meanwhile, one of the clock's hands had swept eighty per cent already.

He had two options with him- either to embrace spirituality or to tour the world and make it aware of the value of limited precious time everyone has.

He had chosen the world tour. He wanted to give his idea of a clock to the world.

He roamed all around the world, preaching about the wonder clock. He told everyone that all of us had it in our minds. The animals turned a deaf ear to his advice, but the humans took the idea and prospered leaps and bounds.

Anyone who respects time prospers in this world. Dadu told me.

The story had ended, but the message was quite clear to me.

"I will respect time from now on". I told Dadu and started to devote my time to the homework at once.

My mother came to Dadu's room.

"Ron! Your bus services to school has been resumed". She informed me and went on to perform household chores.

I gazed at the hourglass placed above the cupboard of Dadu's room.

Dadu had gifted me an hourglass on my birthday. It was quite same as the clock embedded into peculiar rabbit's chest. Now, I could appreciate the value of that gift. Time is precious and must be respected. I thought for a while.

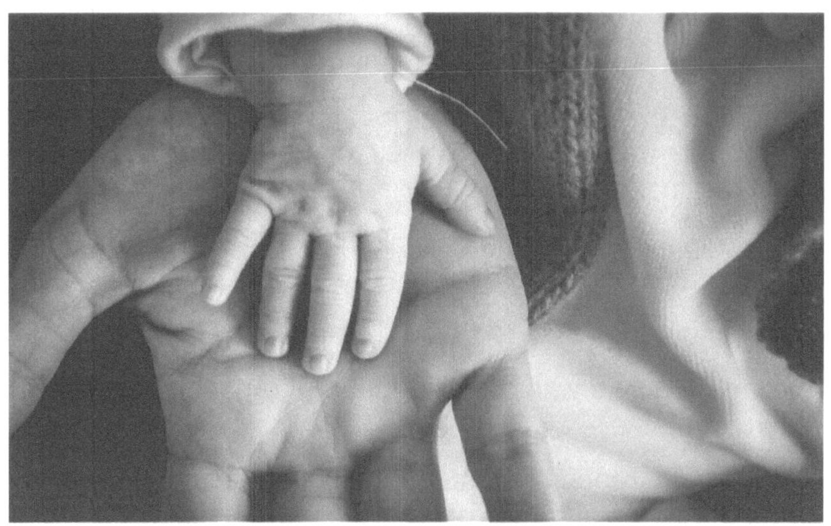

8. **Love your mom! Forgive your father**

The snow at the peak of shiwaliks had melted away. The pastel white summits had been turned into chocolate brownie

hardened with pride.

Dadu nudged my shoulder softly to wake me up. It was a way surprising to me as I was accustomed to mother's ultimatums with a final tight slap every now and then in the morning.
The clock had struck 5 A.M. In our modern era, even the cocks crow very late in the morning, i.e., the usual Cucko-doo-koo. Perhaps, they too know that the Humans have the luxury of alarm clocks now.

"Dadu! Can I have some more sleep?" I tossed again, away from his side. Dadu denied my request.

If I would have croaked like this to my father; the result would have been a tight slap exactly like a missile manoeuvering into its predestined target.

Meanwhile, both of us set out for a walk to the park; though a bit late. It was a pleasant Sunday morning.

Samosas at the confectioner shops were dancing in Kadai. Grocers were ready to greet their customers with a humble smile in the market.

Grass alongside the roads had clothed in lush green. On the way, Dadu also offered prayers at the temple.

"What would we do next?" I asked Dadu.

"Trekking," He said with a smiling face and gazing towards the mighty mountains.

We will try to reach that summit. He, at once pointed his finger towards the summits of Nag Tibba Mountain.

"But Why?" I questioned him.

"Simply! We will explore and learn; it would help you in your lessons too."

"Also! We will get a little time to discuss about your problems" Dadu said further.

The last sentence was an elixir to my senses and intoxicated my mind.

I thought "If it would be so; I would never study and would only trek on the Nag Tibba summits".

I was fancied with the dreams of becoming a Mowgli that would get graduated to Tarzan later on, fetching myself into the league of the toppers list in my class.

My episodes of daydreaming only helped me to cover the distance from park to home with ease.

"Check all your stuff for trekking!" Dadu told me.

"Yes! I got all of them" I said with excitement.

Backpack, raincoat, polarising sunglasses, walking stick, tent, emergency light, etc. - I had packed all the stuff in no time.

Ron's Best Gifts ever – samar deep singh

I had been to jungle camping with Dadu once. It was surrounded with Sal trees having a river stream alongside. Bonfire and the dance alongwith the fireflies at night had created an awesome experience. But, Guys! Never mind of the mosquitoes there. Even the roses bloom with thorns around it.

Our trail to Nag Tibba had begun. En route, we found gorgeous natural streams, sprawling meadows and some peaks still blanketed with snow but quite far away from us.

Within four hours, we reached our destined summit with finesse. Dadu had named it as 'the summit of love'.He had his best memories with his soulmate here.

"Close your eyes; I have something special for you, "Dadu said.

 I closed the eyes as instructed. My joy knew no bounds when I opened my eyes after a while.

"Wow, Dadu! What a spectacular glimpse of the valley below" I yelled in delight. It was drenched with mighty Alaknanda River that was dancing into its curvy meanders. The picturesque was quite serene and perfect to watch.

"Prepare the tent, Ron!" Dadu ordered me.

Dadu had taken some water from a stream on the trail. With this, He made Maggi using a battery-operated kettle. The taste of Maggi in Delhi and Himalayas is quite different. You can bet! Dadu played the violin for me imitating the lyrics of an old Bollywood song:

"Do lafzon ki hai dil ki kahani.....Ya hai mohabbat ya hai Ravani...lalalalala"

"The perfect combination of music, Maggi and the scenery below the valley were one of the best memories to cherish. It was an awesome experience, far greater than playing a video game at home" I told Dadu in excitement.

"Simple things create beautiful moments of life. Only one has to discover them. Happiness is still free of cost and always will be!" Dadu added further.

After some time, he stopped playing the violin.

"Now tell me about the problems of your life that has been puzzling you," Dadu asked.

"My parents are very nasty, and I don't like them. You are the only one to whom I could talk my heart out" I said with a burdened heart.

Dadu smiled a little and opened his purse.

"See! What I have for you? It's a photograph of your parents. Isn't it?"

"Yes! It is" I noticed it without any expression on my face.

"Listen! I love my mom so much, but my father scolds me very often. I don't like his attitude."

"I've got a solution for you," Dadu said to me.

"Take this photograph of your parents and throw it down this valley" I gazed at Dadu in surprise. I took a photograph and thought a bit.

"I can't throw my mom's photograph" I reverted to Dadu instantly.

"Mothers are so dear to all of us. Her irrelevant superstitions surpass all the scientific theories. Even Newton would have thrown his apple onto his head and the Great Einstein would have got puzzled by the mom's logic. In spite of all this, a mother is always special to every child" I thought for a while.

"Can I tear it into half and throw my father's photograph only?" I asked.

Dadu got a bit angry. I can sense his face depicting every emotion of surprise and anger.

"Will you throw my son's photograph?" Dadu questioned.

"I would not let you do that" He smiled a bit after a while.

I said nothing. I was still holding my parents' photograph.

A pin-drop silence was disturbed by a sudden rustling of the wind.

"If you can't even do so, then just accept them as they are!" Dadu told me.

Suddenly the clouds around the valley drew darker, and the air added more velocity. The picturesque around the valley was somehow got erased in no time.

Dadu grew impatient. I sensed the tensed face of Dadu.

"Ron! It's a thunderstorm approaching us and we need to hurry. So pack up fast" Dadu commanded.

I packed all the assets. All of a sudden, the calmness of the serene environment was about to turn into a calamity.

"Ron!, the path through which we had come would take longer, as the thunderstorm would get intensified within an hour and there would be no escape for us then," Dadu said in a bit tensed voice. Ron felt a bit restless too.

Any soul irrespective of age can sense the harm to itself. Ron who was fed up with his life still wanted to live; maybe for one another day. He was still ready to fight for it right now.

Psychology of human mind in a natural disaster and the same in case of depression are two different things. Nobody suffering from depression wants to end his life in a natural disaster.

I could sense Dadu's restlessness too, by now.

"Don't worry. I knew a cave; just a hundred metres away from this summit. Hope it would help us in our escape from the thunderstorm" Dadu said.

"Is it a good idea?" I thought for a while.

I have heard of some stories of Yeti living in the caves at the Nag Tibba summits.

Nevertheless, we went inside the cave.

It was so dark there and fear was gripping my heart tremendously.

The cave was full of spiders, bats, birds and skeletons. It had convinced me that the horror stories that I had heard could be true.

But, still Dadu; unaware of the local stories had advised me to move ahead and explore the cave.

"Who would save me after him in case, the yeti harms Dadu?" I started praying for Dadu's long life.

He beamed the emergency light. It helped me discover a heap of straw. At once, I pounced onto it to find a place to rest for some time.

But, my haste and inexperience had resulted into my doom.

I stumbled down into a pit. Even, Dadu got through into it. He couldn't understand the scenario as everything happened so fast.

In the morning, both of us found ourselves in a truck surrounded by some workers.

One of them told Dadu that there is a tunnel construction going on and that both of us were found unconscious on safety pads.

They had also explained that it was dug through the cave to clear the passage of tunnel and some safety pads were erected over it placing some heap of straw above it as a cushion, to avoid any accident. Dadu thanked all of them for saving their life.

One of them drove us to the nearby highway. It would make our journey to home quite safer. Also, there were no signs of a thunderstorm in the sky. The clear weather welcomed us.

We waited for the bus near a milestone.

In the meantime, Dadu got into his usual philosopher mode.

"How would you have saved yourself if I was not there at the summit?" He asked me.

"Well, I can't imagine myself without you". I reciprocated instantly.

"Father is the best guide in your life. He always try to lessen the pain of your journey through his vast experience. Mother will help you to make the path easier and more comfortable so that you could attain success. Your parents are the only secret to attain success in your life". He enlightened me.

"So, never confront any of them. Just talk to them, they will always give you a way out, whenever you get stuck in your life" He enlightened me with his wise words furthermore.

Another interesting concept I wanted to share with you.

"Get your own hourglass" I obeyed instantly.

Dadu placed it alongside with that of his own, having lesser sand than that of mine.

"The sand in your hourglass is more than ours. The sand depicts time and the hourglass is similar to our life" Dadu enlightened me further.

"The tragedy of our life is that we all have a limited time here. Your parents will not be with you forever. Their Sand depicts that they have lesser time than that of yours."He said while glancing at the two hourglasses kept abreast alongside the highway.

"So,Dear Ron! Love your mother and forgive your father. Hug them truly, deeply and madly" Dadu said in a soft tone.

"To the Mall road", the bus conductor howled from the bus, that stopped at the milestone.

We boarded it to our destination.

It was bedtime.

"Sleep with me," Dadu asked me. I imagined Dadu's eyes to be some sort of magnifying glass that can simplify life's complexities in a lucid way. I am fortunate to scan through this magnifying glass anytime over my problems to find the solutions.

"No! I am going to sleep with my parents" I smiled and left him.

Ron   **Parents**

VIOLIN
The Third Gift.....

Life is like playing a violin solo in public and learning the instrument as one goes on.

Samuel Butler

9. Mysterious girl from Andaman
10. A Cursed Violin
11. Technical Bermuda triangle

9. Mysterious girl from Andaman

A morning walk at Dehradun surrounded by the scenic peaks

of the Shivalik was a mesmerizing experience. Friendly smiling faces of local citizens, top ridge view of the peaks and breath-taking scenery of the landscape made it more awesome. With Dadu! It had become a routine.

Since a week, we had noticed something unusual. There was no sight of house sparrows around the earthen pot filled with water in my courtyard. It had invoked an environmentalist in me.

The vultures had already been declared extinct at Dehradun. I missed the melodious chirping sound of the sparrows around the trees. The pigeon feed at the Lal chowk remained unused these days. I couldn't trace a single pigeon feeding at the Lal chowk while having frequent market visits.

I remember flocking away the feeding pigeons at Lal chowk and loved to disturb them at every visit. It was my favourite pastime. Although, it irritated Dadu very much.

In the meantime, a girl had joined our class as a new admission at school. She sat beside me. But, she looked a bit shy and confused. I saw a tattoo of three birds on her left wrist.

Her long hair was made into two plaits, worn tightly with maroon ribbons. She wore Maroon and white checks divided skirt with an off-white shirt.

The class teacher called our rolls.

"Roll no. 28" She yelled twice.

No response from anyone in the class, irritated her a bit.

"Listen! You,at the last bench, the extreme corner" She pointed her finger towards her.

"Are you new to the class? Your roll no. is 28. Please introduce yourself to all of us." She said.

She stood up and paused for a while. After a few seconds, she uttered -"Ki...a...ra..from Andaman."

The whole class laughed at her.

The teacher shouted at the class to maintain pin-drop silence.

"Do you stammer?" The teacher asked her.

"Yes! Miss." She replied after another pause.

"It's ok. It happens. Don't worry; you will get better with time. Please be seated."She told her in a soft tone.

Two weeks had elapsed. She was regular to the class. But, she never talked to anyone of us. Only a word 'Yes! Miss.' could be heard from her during the roll calls.

Her activities got mysterious with time. She was nicknamed as 'Miss mysterious' by the class. She developed a strange behaviour which became evident to the whole school in no time.

Once, I saw her talking to the wall during recess, near the school compound. I gazed at her with surprise. After she had finished talking for a few minutes, she moved to my side and saw me. But, she sneaked out quietly to the class without a single expression on her face.

She could be seen everywhere that we can't approach. Terrace, fences and the park which had a prohibited tag were her favourites. Sometimes she could be seen talking to the sky facing her head towards it, during the recess or sports game period. Her activities had made our class famous. She had become a hot topic of gossips at the school. Everybody knew our class and nicknamed it as the class of 'Miss mysterious'.

Memes on the social media groups were full of edited photographs about her. In those memes, she could be seen talking to the ghosts. She could also be seen talking to Christ in one of the pictures and He would tell her to count more stars in the daytime. Someone took her photograph and edited it by placing the Christ in the sky at the top of the page.

Once we found her sitting above the school compound terrace with legs facing towards the ground. One student called the principal. She was furious at her.

Nobody knew what the punishment she got was!

Rumours spread that she could count the stars and even track the constellations at daytime. Students began to question her curiously. Some girls asked her as to how many stars she had counted so far.

"Have you talked to the ghosts today?" One student asked her.

It became a frequent question that she came across. She didn't respond to any questions and kept her calm.

October 10th - It was her birthday. The whole school knew it and was super excited. Every student mocked her by enacting as if they were talking to the wall. Everywhere she went, the entire school mocked her by pointing fingers towards the sky. Nevertheless, everyone wished her later on her birthday. It was the best hilarious day at school.

Next day, the annual day function rehearsals were started. She took part in singing Christmas carols also.

In the auditorium, she took the mike and spoke to all of us.

"Hello everyone, attention please!"

All the students were stunned and amazed. Miss Mysterious could speak as well.

"Thanks, guys, for the birthday wishes. You were all nice and amazing. I liked your mocking stuff yesterday. Sorry to all of you for myself being alone and not talking to anyone of you.I will try to be familiar to all of you." She stopped then.

All the students in the auditorium clapped for her and laughed their heart out.

So, that's how I have got a new friend. Next day, the whole school saw her in a different avatar. She was talking to everyone like a free bird that chirps without a cause. She whispered a story into my ears during the class, for which the teacher had scolded her twice. Everyone in the class laughed at this.

One day, after the rehearsals, we heard that our school bus will arrive late.

So, we waited for the bus outside our school campus.

"With whom do you talk to every day?" I questioned her frankly.

"To the birds" She replied after a pause that surprised me a bit.

"Could you call them for me?" I asked her.

 She was quiet again.

"I knew you were joking to me" I pretended to laugh at her.

"Hello, I am Mr Harry Potter. I could fly with my broom. Today, I forgot my wand and broom. As you know, they were strictly prohibited in the school premises." I boasted to her.

She closed her eyes and chanted loudly for a few minutes.

Within seconds, I saw the birds flocked and lined up on the terrace of the school compound facing us all around the corner and on the ground.

"Tomorrow, get your wand and broom. I would like to see them." She walked away, leaving me alone. The birds also flew away in no time.

One month had elapsed since she attended school. Her absence made a flurry of messages and edited photographs on social media, once again. One had posted a picture in which she was in the lap of a ghost. Another meme had her photograph with the Christ with a caption-"Come to me, my child; you have counted enough stars at daytime."

But, I was worried. I came up to Dadu's room and discussed the matter with him.

"Dadu, I had a friend. She hadn't come to the class for a month. I am afraid that she might be sick or in some acute problems. She stays all alone in the city. We must go and find her." I told him.

Next day, He met with the principal and got her address. The quest of Kiara had begun.

We reached near a big bungalow in the outskirts of Dehradun. It was in its ruins and looked rather haunted. But, the presence of numerous birds and the loud chirping sound everywhere around the bungalow confirmed me of her presence.

"It seemed all the birds of Dehradun flocked here for a feast," Dadu told me in surprise.

We entered the premises. It was full of birds. I tried to recognize some of the them- House sparrows, crested serpent eagle, Rock pigeon, crested kingfisher, rose ring parakeet, etc. From sofa set to the floor, everywhere I could find the birds.

We went upstairs and found her busy with the House sparrows. They looked dull and half unconscious. I counted twenty of them sitting on her lap.

"What's wrong with these birds? It seemed that you have hosted a ball for them" Dadu enquired her in surprise.

" Sir, I am a resident of Havelock Islands, Andaman. We run a vet hospital and an NGO to cure and preserve the birds. Once, a vulture flew to us, but it had died even after we could cure it. We found that it was affected by a virus.

We have studied the reports of Indian media about the rapid extinction of vultures. The same virus had affected the house sparrows. I had given the anti-virus serum to most of them and even those unaffected. It will keep them resistant to the virus. But those who got already affected must be treated soon. I was planning to take these birds away to the Andaman".

"But how would you transport them to such a far distance?" Dadu asked in surprise.

"We have to find a solution; otherwise, these birds would die. Have you called all the birds that were affected by the virus and left untreated?" Dadu asker her.

"Yes, sir!" She said with a rare smile on her face.

Next day, we hired a big truck and set out towards south India.

But, the police at Doon national park caught us with the truck and handed us over to the conservative forest officer.

We told him the whole story. He didn't accept our claims. He had taken all the birds into his custody.

He also lodged an FIR against three of us. He said that he would hand us over to the police with the charges of theft. Another charge was that we were heading towards Delhi to sell the birds illegally. We found ourselves confined in a lock-up room.

Next day, Kiara called up the officer. She urged him once again that the birds were sick and need immediate treatment. The officer denied her request and laughed at her.

She fainted in the lock-up room after an hour. Dadu told the officer to help her reach the hospital, failing which; he said that he would complain torturing the girl in the lock-up. The officer got a bit confused and came to our terms after some hesistation.

She got hold of the officer at once and smeared a white powder on his face that made him unconscious at once. This act surprised both of us.

"What was that?" We both asked her at a time.

"Don't worry! He will be all right after an hour. The powder will make him forget the incidents of at least past a month". She told us while washing her hands at the lavatory.

"How much time would he take to recover?" Dadu asked her.

"Around a month, till we reach Andaman along with the birds". She told us with a killer smile.

We were amazed at her prompt action.

We snatched the officer's badge and the office seal. We took a special ambulance, meant to transport sick animals of the national park. We opened the birds' vault at the national park. It had many birds that were about to be smuggled across the nation illegally. We identified our sick house sparrows.

Kiara removed the tag around the cages and set them free. We put our house sparrows in the ambulance.

Dadu drove the ambulance.

"It would lead us safely to the shores," He told us with a smile on his face.

Kiara and I fed the birds in the meantime.

After a journey of three days, we reached to the shores of Andhra Pradesh. She told us to stop the ambulance at Lover's fort near the Sunset point.

Finally, we reached our destination. Kiara was happy to see the fort. It was flocked with numerous pigeons. We were amazed again. But, I observed Dadu being a little bit worried.

"What next from here?" He asked Kiara.

"Don't Worry. Both of you had done enough for me and the sick house sparrows" Kiara told us, being happy & content this time.

"Did you see pigeons at the fort? They were rock pigeons from Andaman. We chose, fed and trained them for a special purpose. Have you heard of the pigeon post? They act as our pigeon ambulance at our Island" She enlightened us further.

"In ancient times, the pigeons used to carry messages and possess natural homing abilities. They were called as homing pigeons and quite good at remembering their respective homes. Also, good at finding their way, even when they've been transported distances, far away from home" Dadu added further, increasing my knowledge as always.

"Why did you choose them? Once my pet pigeon flew away and never came back" I told her.

"Pigeons always fly home. They have magneto receptive skills. It means that they can detect and orient towards magnetic fields. They could move to accurate distances." she added with a smile.

She had many specialized canisters in her bag. We kept the house sparrows in the canisters and attached it later on with the pigeons, to transport them to the destination. She flew all of them. They got disappeared to the horizon after some time.

It was sunset, and we boarded the ship to Havelock Island, Andaman.

Why couldn't we got them transported along with us?" I asked Dadu curiously while on the journey.

"It is illegal to transport them as per the government laws." He said.

Next, we reached to Havelock Island. You could call it the 'Island of Birds'. A mile away we saw a board. It read:

Havelock bird NGO & vet hospital- Save the birds. Save nature.

Dadu appreciated her work along with the volunteers on the Island. It was amazing that none of the birds flew away, on our approach towards them. I have taken selfies with every bird around.

She was pleased to see both of us at her residence.

After two days, we returned to the fort near sunset point at Andhra Pradesh and took the same ambulance to reach Doon national park. We parked it at the entrance.

The officer was amazed to see us. But, he didn't recognize us.

"You have forgotten your ambulance on the highway," Dadu told him.

"Yes! I have memory issues these days" We smiled and left to our home.

Next day, we set out for the routine morning walk. I could see the pigeons at the Lal chowk being fed. Some house sparrows had also returned to our courtyard for water. I could listen to the chirping of the birds in the morning. The music gifted by nature had come alive.

Dadu had said once – "Music must not leave our life."

"I can connect it with the Dadu's violin." I thought for a while.

10. A cursed violin

Ron's Best Gifts ever – samar deep singh

The ice-cream pact was still alive between us. It was started when I was in Nursery class. Dadu had chronic diabetes and the sweets were strictly banned for him in the house

After the school, Dadu accompanies me throughout the way back to home. We enjoy our favourite ice-cream

At home, I used to smuggle sweets to his room, from the fridge. That pact had encapsulated our relation into a steel frame. None of us reveals anything about this to my parents.

"Old age is such an epitome of stories that never end. Retirement and childhood are complementary to each other. One, having the experience and the other with layers of inexperience and immaturity. Truly, one balances the other" Dadu had enlightened me once.

Dehradun is completely covered with snow. Nature is having an ice cream pact with the mother earth.

One morning, I had a serious quarrel with my parents. I threatened them that I would leave home one day if they keep scolding me like this every now and then. Later on, I came to my Dadu's room.

It was Sunday. So, we planned to have a ride.

We were on the verge of having another set of ice-cream pact. But, on the way; we met with a minor accident. One biker had nudged the left side of our bike. The biker got very angry and abused Dadu.

Though, it was not our mistake; Dadu said sorry to him, even after hearing him abuse.

My nerves lost temper, but Dadu alluded me to keep quiet. I felt that I was like the fourth monkey of Dadu.

See no evil, hear no evil, speak no evil and the last one is myself - the monkey that was asked to ignore everything. A similar plight of every common man in the nation now-a-days.

"Your wounds would not heal by abusing and slapping others" He added further.

"That's why Mahatma Gandhi advised offering another cheek if someone slaps us," I said in such a low tone that he ignored.

Meanwhile, we rushed to the nearby hospital. He had minor bruises at knee and forehead. The doctor had advised him for a week's rest.

Old age needs a companion. The best gift that you can give them is your precious time. The same scenario is true for children also.

Next day, I went to his room. His face was not so vibrant. I started gazing at the photo-albums dangled at the walls. He loves to tell stories connected with his life. Getting into his room is like picking a book and reading it, at a vast library. You will never know which one gets to your side.

A spontaneous question crept into my mind.

"Can I ask you something?" I asked him.

"Yes, Dear!" He replied to me, ignoring the pain.

"Physical wounds could be healed through medicines. How the mental wounds around your heart could be healed? That man, who abused you, had disturbed my mind since then. But, you ignored him who abused you so harshly?

I also, used to get angry just when my classmates make fun of me about my lacklustre performance in studies and frequent bashing by the teachers. It hurts me a lot". How to deal with all this stuff? I asked him in a low tone.

A pin-drop silence covered the room. He gazed at the portrait of his wife and then moved slightly to my side.

"Ah! You have set the right tone. It's a good question, though!" He said in a low voice.

"Music and hobby are the two best approaches to heal yourself," he told me.

"They are not an instant elixir to fetch you instant relief. But, both work well in due course of time. Both lessens the pain.

 What could have a heart achieved on this earth if it hadn't danced to the tunes of music or at least involved itself in a hobby? It kindles hope and confidence in our heart. Time and hobby are two great healers." He enlightened me further.

Dadu paused for a minute and started again with a smile on his face. He was about to open another page of his life's memories.

"It was a gala time for all of us when your mother informed us that she was having a baby. Ron! It was you. We were on cloud nine. Your father had just gone crazy. He distributed sweets to every person he knew in the town.

But, it was the eighth month of your mother's pregnancy. She was diagnosed with dengue and her platelets count started depleting insanely. It was the life threat for you and your mother.

Our hopes of any recovery were dwindling with time. One day your heart-beat stopped. She cried madly in front of the doctor.

"What would be the meaning of my life without my son's heartbeat?" She yelled to the nurse and it was the prime reason for her mourning then.

As a family, we all have nothing left in our hands except for consoling her.

Meanwhile, the doctor came. She tried very hard to overcome the situation.

Hope is an elixir and it works brilliantly. He continued.

"Jahnvi, you have to live at least for the sake of your baby." The doctor yelled at your mother.

She gave a series of injections to your mother afterwards. After a while, the sound of your heart-beat revived.

The doctor yelled to your mother- "Hey! Listen to his heart-beat" The moment she heard your heart-beat and smiled, we had a sigh of relief. The doctor had just brought an ultrasound machine and placed it near her bed. She attached the cables close to her ears.

"Listen to your son's heartbeat. You are his only hope; so that he could come into this world. Don't lose hope. Everything would be fine" The doctor added further.

That lub-dub sound of heart-beat had sent ripples of happiness into the whole family. We listened to that sound again and again, as if we were just playing with you.

That sound of your heart-beat was the best music created by the God that time. After a few days, she recovered and gave birth to you."

That true story of my birth had garnered immense respect for my mother and love for my father.

Tears rolled out of my eyes; unintentionally; just like the foam above the coffee cup. To top it, I imagined two hearts; one for my father and another for my mother.

"How mean I was; that I had threatened them saying I would leave home one day. How rude was my behaviour with them?" I cursed myself.

Dadu understood my feelings. He patted me and opened another chapter of his life.

"Ron! Our freedom struggle was much hard-fought. We Satyagrahis' knew the meaning of that very well."

I gave him a surprised look.

"Were you a Satyagrahi?" I asked him curiously.

He nodded into a big 'Yes'.

"A mere utterance of Vande Mataram enabled all of us to sustain heavy blows of lathi-charge done by the Britishers."

"Is the music so powerful?" I questioned him again.

"Yes, my son!" He smiled a little.

"It kindles fire to our passion and targets."

Dadu chanted further a famous Bollywood patriotic song:

Sarfaroshi ki tamanna ab hamare dil me hai

Dekhna hai jor kitna baju-e-qatil ....me hai

The song even swelled my heart with pride, kindling the feelings of patriotism in me. Now, I could relate everything, he said.

A pin-drop silence was there in the room for quite a while. Dadu started looking at his wife's photograph.

Suddenly a question peeped through my mind.

"Where have you learnt the violin?" I enquired.

"It's a long story, Ron!" Sighed my Dadu.

"I am all ears. My sweet Dadu!" I told him again. He was about to open another chapter of his life.

"Your grandmother was a veteran in playing the violin. She used to play it every now and then. In those days, I used to ridicule her multiple times; for being busy with my office work, even when at home. The sound of violin irritated me a lot.

Money sometimes erodes the sense of appreciating pleasures of life. It kills creativity and the art of admiring simple things. Earning money had become the only pleasure for me at that time. Every other work was useless to me.

On one fateful evening, your grandmother had got a paralysis stroke. It was a double impact in her suffering.

She already had a chronic migraine.

 Perhaps, she used to play the violin to lessen her pain by drifting her concentration away from her illness. I understood that very late.

The stroke had weakened her hands. She couldn't play the violin any more. She was into her worst painful days. Her suffering was unbearable to me. I wanted to make her happy and relaxed.

One day I took her violin and started playing it for her.

"She smiled at first. You are terrible at music, dear!" She told me.

By the way, I enjoyed her smile.

I continued playing the violin frequently for her; just to lessen her pain and suffering to some extent.

With time, that made me a veteran in playing the violin too.

After some time, she passed away on one nasty Friday evening. But, I used to retrospect into her thoughts through music. It drew me closer to her. It lessens my pain of losing her to some degree." His voice shrivelled as he ended.

"I didn't want to hurt you, Dadu," I said with grief.

I wiped Dadu's tears. I took the violin and started playing it.

He started smiling. That day, I came to know that the inner wounds could be healed through a hobby. And that, Music is one of them. There is no need to show aggression as we are habituated to do so, quite frequently.

I started engaging myself in taking lessons to play the violin; from Dadu for the same purpose.

11. Technical Bermuda Triangle

It's a common phenomenon or rather a cultural aspect in Indian families to point out all the fingers at the youngest child in the family if anything in the home goes missing or broken or disturbed from its usual place.

Ron's Best Gifts ever – samar deep singh

The Lord Ganesha statue housed inside the altar, in the drawing-room got slightly disturbed to the south direction. All the sweets went missing for a week. Mother declared me as a culprit without evidence. The flower pot kept at one of the extreme corners of the drawing-room fell onto the floor last night. It disturbed her a lot. She was furious at me.

I installed a CCTV camera in the drawing-room and monitored the activities for two days but failed to catch the culprit. I took the remote-controlled robot car toy and attached a video camera to search the culprit at all the corners of my house.

I found a cat hidden in our storehouse with two kittens. I showed the video to the whole family. They laughed at the video and later on, we added the three-member cat family into ours.

Dadu was impressed with me. He told me that I should always find ways to use the technology for a good cause and that I must not overwhelm myself in the gadgets that waste my time and hamper my studies.

It was 10 o'clock already. Perfect time for another bedtime story by Dadu.

"Dear Ron, it was the story of a boy named 'Steve' from a well-off family. I would like to tell the story in Steve's words itself" Said Dadu and thus continued.

"I dwell at the plush mansion - the Verma's. My father was the head of Artificial intelligence department at the University of Allahabad. He was also a pioneer in home automation technology and had a successful business venture in this field. My mother actively participated in my father's business ventures. Both were quite busy with their career.

I always felt blessed as a proud resident of this mansion. Complete home automation was done by my parents. Smart lighting systems, Smart video technology with 4k displays & High-Definition video-cum-sound system in every room was the major attraction of the mansion. Latest Home security devices were installed to take care of every nook and corner of the house. I had every gadget in my room to comfort my life.

I had harnessed all of them to my prime advantage.

My friends felt privileged to visit the mansion. They went awestruck by the luxuries of life and the latest gadgets in my house.

It's five o'clock in the morning. The alarm clock rang and vibrated to its full enthusiasm to awaken me.

It said - "Good morning, Steve".

The phablet at my bedside popped up – "You have twenty notifications regarding your friends at social media platforms and three from your school with one requiring an urgent response."

"Stupid, don't ever recall me about the school's notifications. I hated it." I acted to be a bit furious at that sweet female voice. But, honestly speaking; I loved that.

"Sure, Mr Steve," The phone's assistant said in a sweet voice.

After a few minutes, the laptop switched on in an auto mode and popped up its notifications.

"Do you want to listen to your appointments scheduled for today, Mr Steve?"

"Yes sure, Caran; please tell me," I said in a sweet voice to the virtual assistant of my laptop.

School   7:30 AM - 2:30 PM

Parent- teachers meeting 3:00 PM

You have chosen to complete the play station level 4 (video game) today at 6:00 PM for an hour.

You have to make the notes and complete the homework that was pending for two days. Your school had already marked a red flag on that. That will hamper your grades further.

A Birthday party of your classmate is scheduled at 8:00 PM."

"Ok, I got it. Now, shut off the system. Remind me again, when I reach home back after school in the evening. Don't ever tell me the consequences. I'm your boss." I told him.

"Sorry sir" Caran the virtual assistant got silent after a sorry message.

I stepped inside my car. "Where do you want to commute, sir?" Another virtual assistant in the car nicknamed Peter; asked me about my preferences.

"Stupid, don't you know where I have to commute every day? To the school of course and for your kind information" I replied it in a harsh tone.

"Sorry, sir" Peter replied to me very politely.

"I don't want any men's voice. Replace it with the sweet women's tone." I told Peter in a bit harsh voice.

"Nice sir, please test Ela's voice."

"Welcome sir" A sweet, soft and comfy lady's voice was heard.

"Yeah, it's so soothing to my ears. Please keep that."

"Thanks, sir; happy to help you from now on" Ela responded swiftly.

The car stopped at my school's coordinates.

"Ela, don't park the car here. Mom needs it at her office. Please pick her from the office to the Shopping Mall."

She accepted my orders. I stepped out of the car and moved towards the school campus.

The driverless car swiftly headed towards my mother's office coordinates.

Meanwhile, I entered my school premises.

"Open your digital pods and show me your homework," The teacher asked all the students of my class.

The AI robot beside the teacher checked everyone's Homework. It raised a Red flag at my homework. It indicated that it was not my original draft.

"Steve, your homework seemed to be completed by a virtual assistant. It's not your original draft. Can't you apply your own mind?" The teacher was furious at me.

"It was your last warning. Next time, I will send notifications to your parents." She added further. The robot that checked my homework looked at me with a smile.

I popped up my virtual assistant that helped in my school activities. I nicknamed it as 'Hayes'.

"Hello, what can I do for you? The Virtual classroom assistant is at prompt notice for you anytime." Hayes added further.

"Stupid, what was that? You can't even do my homework correctly! Just listen and record today's lecture. I got a 'C' grade today and a red flag too. I would tell my father to decrypt your program files afresh.

The teacher also announced that our yearly exams would be conducted in the last week of this month.

Meanwhile, a girl came to our class via a scholarship from a remote village. I was consistently a backbencher. She sat right along with me on the bench. I hadn't noticed anything special about her.

She doesn't even have a laptop to study at the class.

Her dress and grooming didn't reflect the convent school standards. She had a very short haircut and wore a sky blue band with a set of small blue round studs in the ear lobes.

She had applied the henna and blue nail polish that was strictly prohibited in the school. She would certainly get a bashing from our class teacher soon.

But, she was quite sharp at every subject. She stood up every time the teacher asked a question in the class throughout the day. Her name was Shanaya.

Next day, at school; I asked her for a favour.

"Could you help me with my homework? How could I draft it virtual assistant free?" I asked her.

"Analyze by your heart and apply your mind." She replied in a sweet voice. It was much sweeter than the virtual assistant 'Ela'. I could bet with anyone.

"You have to write about the feelings that you have for your mother. I 'm sorry, No robot or virtual assistant could draft that one. What kind of a son you are, if u cannot write a paragraph about your mother?" She cross-questioned me again.

From the past one year, I had not met my mother except on video conferencing sessions. She looked like a virtual mother to me by now. Nanny nurtured my childhood.

 I was so confused during my childhood, as to whom I should address 'Nanny' and whom to call 'mummy'.

I couldn't get much emotional bonding with her.

Shanaya gave me an important lesson of life that was a hundred per cent correct.

I reached home quite late. It was the time for play station 4 (video game). It was quite a secretive affair. I had a drone at the exit of the house to watch any activity of my parents approaching the house. It was rare but, no excuses as they might catch me red-handed.

In case of such casualty, the video game will change itself into an interactive math tutorial.

It's a program manipulated by me. My parents were very busy with their career & business. They talked to me via a ten-minute video conference every weekend. Although, any grave issue could be reported to them within seconds by raising notifications or video calling.

Meanwhile, Shanaya was quite comfortable to sit with me on the last bench.

I found it quite advantageous to share the seat with her. My virtual assistant doesn't like it. Maybe some jealousy code crept into its program. She helped me in every subject.

The yearly exams had approached in no time. I hadn't revised much. I set out from my home to the examination hall.

I questioned the Robot on my car's left side that had the supercomputer characteristics. "Please process the data of my mind and let me know as how much could I score in the exam?"

It kept its two prongs at my forehead. It calculated a strict ninety-nine per cent failure chances.

"What was the rest one per cent chance?" I enquired further.

"Only if your father could plant a virus into the exam software to corrupt it. It will delay itself to get you more time for your studies."

"It was quite impossible, I thought for a moment. Why would my father do that?" I thought for a moment.

Nevertheless, I had appeared for the exam and it was miserable.

Next week, I joined the classes. Shanaya looked a bit tensed. I asked her the reason for the same.

"My grandmother is not well. She had an accident last year" She told me in a sad tone.

Helping a girl in adversity is every boy's dream. I am not an exception.

We took special permission from the principal to leave the school premises.

"How did you come to know about your grandmother's illness?" I asked her.

"Telegram" She replied softly.

"What? I thought the telegram in India had got obsolete." I was surprised a bit.

"No, dear friend. India is still a developing nation." She replied promptly.

She insisted to me to drive my car.

"No! It's driverless and automatic. Just have a seat. Tell it the coordinates of your grandmother's residence. The car starts only through my biometric scans. It could only be handed over to my father or the police in case of theft." I told her proudly.

"Nelson Street" She voiced softly and hinted the co-ordinates thereafter.

Ela, the Car's assistant welcomed us in a sweet tone. It drove us to her Grand Mother's residence coordinates swiftly.

We reached the village in an hour. Her grandmother was quite surprised by our presence. We too were a little bit surprised to see her at the entrance. It was some sort of prank by the old lady that I imagined. "She might not have been bedridden." I thought for a while.

"Your parents didn't come?" She inquired at once to Shanaya.

"I haven't informed them. I came upon my own with my best friend. I was so worried about you." She replied to her grandmother in a sweet tone.

"You have grown up, darling." The Grandmother kissed her. It was really the most precious emotion that I missed for years. The last time my parents had done so; was when I got bedridden two years back.

She had cooked favourite dishes for her. "Even my birthday was celebrated through video conferencing this year. Not to mention the dishes." I thought again.

Her grandmother told me about Shanaya's childhood pranks. She blushed at it.

Ron's Best Gifts ever – samar deep singh

At night, we went to the terrace and watched the stars in the sky and fireflies on the ground. It was a mesmerizing experience apart from my Hi-tech life.

She made me learn how to track and identify the constellations. The 'dipper' was my favourite. We played shadow movements. No need to control the AC temperature and humidity settings here. Nature is at work. Everything was so simple but exciting.

The handmade cake came. It was Shanaya's birthday. I started my drone. It hovered above us and took the photographs of the precious moments of the celebration.

So how do you study? She asked me as we have to complete our homework.

I opened all the accessories from my bag. It was the Pod, Phablet & laptop; then commanded all the virtual assistants to help me with the homework. Shanaya looked a bit surprised at this.

"Shut them all. You need only a copy and pen to study. Try to pen your homework in your own words. Concentrate and revise as many times as you can; afterwards. Don't make simple things so complicated. It will confuse you. She enlightened me like a boss.

For example, for the mother's essay; think about nice events related to your mother. Use short sentences and write in your own words." She explained.

I woke up at sharp four in the morning. No need of alarms here. Circadian rhythm of my body worked fine. Within a few minutes, Shanaya's grandmother came to wake us up. She kissed us later on and packed the tiffin for both of us. She gifted a handmade doll and sweater as a birthday gift to Shanaya.

We left to school in the car. It was a mesmerizing experience.

The first time, I missed my parents a lot. The virtual world and the technology can't match with parent's kiss, love and care. I learnt that we can't substitute the personal touch and care to machines.

Next day, I summoned my parents to my room. They behaved like victims to me.

My mother had got wrinkles that were not evident to me at video conferencing. She had great make – up skills. But, the daylight revealed it.

"Sorry, Steve, we were quite busy on a project." Both of them told me simultaneously.

"Is anything more important than me?" I questioned them.

"No!" My parents told me in a soft tone.

"Both of you, Please come and kiss your son. I had missed the touch of my beloved parents. I knew that both of you were busy with your projects. But, I want my share of time and love from both of you."

 Three of us went quite emotional and burst into tears.

Surprisingly, the room's smart lighting system had gone dim. It sensed the emotional environment.

"Dad, I would come to you and will disturb you anytime at my will. It's my right. You can scold me at every mistake of mine. You will get this opportunity very soon as I had written a miserable exam.

Mother, it's your duty to wake me up every morning by kissing on my forehead."

All of us laughed and accepted our mistakes.

"Come, it's evening, let's go for a walk together." My mother asked me.

It seemed that the silence in Steve's life had filled with melodies of love and emotions. I also took Dadu's violin to add some music into my life.

Dadu, it was an awesome story. I told him and kissed thereafter.

He smiled a little and fell asleep within minutes.

MIRROR
The Fourth Gift…

The world is a great mirror. It reflects back to you what you are.

Thomas Dreier

12. A complete Hero
13. The Next Entrepreneur
14. The secret of the smiling Mirror

12. A Complete Hero

One of my childhood dreams was to become a fighter Jet pilot. The photo frame dangled at the extreme left corner of the wall at Dadu's room was the source of my inspiration. He was standing with his fighter aircraft. It showed his intrepid genius & remarkable career.

One day, while I was at the last leg of finishing my homework, Dadu came back from the Shiva temple & sat beside me.

"What were you gazing at, on the wall?" He asked randomly.

"That picture of yours in which you are standing along with a fighter aircraft. I want to be like you. I want to be a hero. Defeating the enemies & downing their aircrafts is one of my dreams." I replied.

"Whatever you are talking about, are not the real attributes of a hero. Heroes are of different genre. You can find them in every field. Just follow your passion & accomplish your aim. If you do so, I would be proud of you." He enlightened me.

"Were you the best fighter pilot of your time?" I asked him another question.

Dadu paused for some time. He smiled at first & it seemed that he was about to recite another chapter of his life.

"Yes, we were one of the best in the business, equipped with the best minds & equipment. I was fortunate to get trained by a real hero. He was the most accomplished & famed fighter pilot of his time. He trained us for a week as a trainer. I had met him only twice. Yet, he was one of my best friends. As for me, I was an average. You could call him a complete hero."

"Dadu, was he more courageous than a superhero. Had he equipped with some sort of superpowers as such?" I asked him curiously.

"World don't need superheroes. We need ourselves to be more courageous & brave. Let's talk about him. It's a true story of a great soldier and a Patriot, I should say".He replied.

Dadu started telling me, the true story of 'a complete Hero'.

The world war one had begun. Germany had overpowered all the nations. It had progressed leaps & bounds.

Mr Rudolf Lee was a fighter pilot of Royal air force. A tall, handsome, blue-eyed & copper brown-haired young man into his prime twenties. He was famous for his female friends at every major city of the nation.

Love & romance was a luxury to him, not a serious business. The Ghost hunter written on his aircraft's tail was his another hallmark signature with a skeleton & two bones across it, engraved with pride & precision by him.

At first, I saw him dating a pretty lady at a restaurant near the base. Both were busy with gossips, ignoring the champagne & red roses. She left after some time.

I approached him towards his table.

"Can I join you, Mr Lee?" I asked him.

"Of course! Please have a seat." He replied politely.

"Why don't you get into a serious relationship with a single girl & marry her?" I asked him with a smile.

"Dear, I am a soldier. I have already got married to my favourite A117 fighter jet aircraft. I will only live & die with it. It is the most advanced & technically equipped aircraft in the world, more romantic & smarter than anyone I could traverse and mingle with. A kind of Love at first sight, I should say. After all of this, I make friends only." Mr Lee explained with a usual killer smile on his face.

During that time, the German air force was a synonym of terror in the sky. It had bombed over three coastal bases of the Royal air force.

The emergency was called on across the nation.

It was late in the evening. The London airbase was also attacked & bombed. I was attending a training session at the same airbase. The loud bombing sound had shattered the glasses on window panes around our residence.

An Emergency hooter announced:

"Attention! It was a probable attack by the German air force. It was a surprise military airborne attack without any prior warning. All the pilots & cadets are requested to assemble at the Emergency meeting room."

 The loud sound reverberated multiple times.

Well, it had ravaged the whole airbase except the A117 jet fighter aircraft, assigned to Mr Lee & three other bomber aircrafts. Only the training camp building, which was our residence had survived. It undermined everybody's morale at the base.

Another report by the hooter at late night gave us Goosebumps.

 "An aircraft laden with 100 KG armour piercing bombs had taken off without approval from the base authorities. An enquiry is under process. Please be alert. Report to the authorities in case of any suspicious activity."

Next day, a news channel had reported from the sources at Berlin airbase, Germany:

An A117 fighter jet aircraft armed with armour piercing bombs attacked our airbase. We had a few casualties. It flew towards the Berlin airbase & our radar tracked it with a befitting reply afterwards. It had destroyed a part of German airbase building & no casualties were reported yet. The pilot was caught & his identification is under progress."

Since then, I had not heard any news about him. Later, another news had confirmed that it was Mr Lee. The tensions among the two formidable air forces remained grim thereafter.

After a decade, I met him at a training session after his retirement. I found him lecturing to the cadets with the same enthusiasm that I had seen in him earlier.

"An organization grows and become strong with values and discipline of its human resource, not with the sophisticated or advanced weaponry and a large number of army personnel in the long run." He continued for quite a long time & later came to train my batch.

He recognized me at once & told me to meet at the restaurant in the evening..

I met him at the same restaurant, where we had met, a decade ago. He was wearing a Gold ring with silver stars embedded at its periphery. I noticed it at the first sight. Well, he tried to hide it.

"Dear, I want to share with you my experiences at the Berlin airbase. It was quite classified. But I trust you. You are the one who told me about the importance of family." He continued with the same killer smile on his face.

When I was captured at the German Air Force base. I thought that I would be imprisoned or executed by them. But, it was altogether, a different world to look at! I pointed my gun to the official who came to search for me.

"Officer! Never point the gun at anything you do not intend to shoot." One of them shouted at me.

I had no option except to surrender. I was admitted to an army hospital.Later on, it came to my knowledge that my favourite aircraft had been crashed by a missile launch from the ground and that I ejected myself safely.

After two days, a European nurse came to me. She checked my pulse & the blood pressure. She greeted me in a local accent that I could not understand.

After some time, an officer came to me & asked about my well-being. I told him my name, rank, social security number & date of birth as per the protocols.

To my surprise, I wasn't arrested, executed or put on trial. After my recovery, I was given an officer's quarter & treated at par with a soldier. I was assigned a mentor to talk to, in case of any issue.

Each time, I asked my mentor as to why they haven't imprisoned or executed me and instead of that, treated me as a soldier with respect. He simply smiled without any comment.

After a few days, I was asked to give a lecture at the school campus, inside the Berlin airbase. About a hundred students were present on the ground.

They all shouted in one voice. "Officer, we hail your courage."

I was awestruck by this gesture. I thought that they would hate me.

I talked to some of the students. A boy even took my autograph & complimented:

"You are so daring, sir."

I cross-questioned him "Who is your superhero?"

"Major Anne Hitchker." I was surprised to know this.

I thought that he would tell any familiar name of superhero or of an actor from leading local cinema.

I roamed around the school. I saw the pictures of martyrs dangled on the walls along with their stories of bravery. Every student knew each one of them, very well.

I was quite surprised that I was not even treated as an enemy alien at the airbase.

I went to the parade ground. I asked the trainer if any rolls had been called for the duty at first.

 "We don't maintain a register. Cadets take no leave. Everybody loves their duty." He told me.

I was free to roam anywhere inside the campus except for the warehouse. I was not even being spied." Mr Lee paused for a while.

"It was an ideal air force base. I learnt from them the leadership traits & how to make an organization strong. They inculcated the feelings of patriotism, courage, integrity & loyalty from the beginning to their generation. I came to know what we lacked.

The best in the business do not fear anyone- Neither God nor the Devil. It was marked on the front gate of the airbase that I missed earlier. It answered all my questions.

I came home as a prisoner of war exchange programme between the two air forces.

On homecoming, I was posted as the head of the Air Force division.

I was received with respect & honour.

But, I could gaze upon the unhappy & jealous faces of my colleagues. Our organization was marred with corruption, indecision, lack of vision & enthusiasm.". He paused for a while.

"In those days, we only relied on our armed forces" I interrupted him a bit.

"I understood why we couldn't match them. We lack values & discipline, in spite of having all weaponry & technical know-how?

I overhauled the system. I took vigorous steps to remove corruption & maintain discipline in my organization. Code of conduct was revised again." He told me.

"In a decade, Royal air force had become a formidable force to reckon due to your efforts & vision." I interrupted him again while complimenting on his services.

"Since then, I train the cadets to instil values in them even after the retirement." He concluded.

That was the last time that I had met him.

It was his sixtieth birthday. I was also invited. He had a celebrity tag across the nation, apart from being the most decorated soldier. I boarded a flight to London.

On my arrival, I came to know about the state of emergency declared all around the nation. A series of terrorist attacks ravaged London. Ten people were reported to be killed. All the passengers were stopped at the airport itself.

An interview of the Prime minister flashed on the screen inside the airport premises.

We hail our hero. He had served the nation at his best. We owe our peace to him. My deepest condolences to the brave heart.

Next morning, the newspaper reports read:

"Hero foiled a possible terrorist attack." A printed photograph was on the right side. I recognized him as Mr Lee.

I drilled the newspaper reports to know how Mr Lee had foiled the attack.

It was said that:

"At the metro, he asked a man to help him with lighting his cigar. But, he refused & ran away. This made him suspicious and Mr Lee tried to catch hold of him.

He caught hold of him somehow & led him outside the station premises by the lift. Just then, unfortunately, that man i.e. the terrorist blew himself.

"You were a complete hero, Mr Lee." Dadu murmured to himself that I heard it too. "

Dadu grew sad while saying so.

"Ron, we don't need superheroes. We need people having courage & bravery that would be sufficient to perform selfless services to the mankind" Dadu continued.

"After six months, a parcel was delivered to my home that had a ring and a letter. That was the same ring which he wore at the meeting then.

The letter had an image of the aircraft with a Ghosthunter mark on its tail.

It read:

"I don't deserve this ring. I tried to have a family with that European nurse. But it didn't work. Anyways, thanks for enlightening me on the importance of a family."

Your friend,

R. Lee

Dadu Concluded.

"Dadu, he was really a complete hero. I'm impressed" I said with excitement..

It was bedtime, I took out the mirror gifted by Dadu, looked into it and exhilarated myself saying "You have to become a real complete hero one day, Ron!"

13. The Next Entrepreneur

It was a unique initiative by our school. Our teachers conducted special evening classes for slum students twice a week. Most of the students of our school volunteered for this social initiative. I wondered if I had any skill left with me.

"Perhaps; nothing"! Then what did I do at school, for such a long time" I thought for a while. Seriously, some of these random thoughts always try to crave my inner self to doom.

Apart from that, every student had to submit a project report about the life and conditions of children at the slum, after the end of sessional exams. We also had to assess their educational and economic conditions.

Our class teacher had divided the class into different zones. Everyone was assigned a particular locality of the slum near our school. I joined that evening class.

The teacher had instructed the class to recite the table of twenty-nine.

A boy among them stood up and recited it in seconds.

I was taken aback by his fluency. The teacher appreciated him. I thought her appreciation was not quite enough. If I would be in lieu of her, then I would have rewarded him with a decent prize.

Reclaiming my Math skills, it was almost like a surgical strike! I could do this stunt up to the table of nine. After that, I have to discover an intelligent body double, desperately for that. Thus, my heart hailed him as a hero immediately and abused myself, a bit as well.

He was Hari. A lean built personality oozing with confidence in his eyes and one of the active participant of the class. The teacher introduced me to him.

He smiled at me. It was the only asset that he had; apart from his Maths acumen. His torn clothes seemed to be stitched multiple times; almost everywhere I could gaze. Our teacher had instructed both of us to keep calm and help each other with the project report.

Drafting a report was a two-way affair. Hari was also required to write a short report about us. Maybe his report will be titled as ' Privileged kids – How they waste resources and opportunities'. From his apparent condition, I came to know how privileged I was; just in comparison to my counterpart.

That night, my family was having dinner. My father had received my sessional marks through a school message. He intimated it to all of us.

"Will you get anything much ahead of 'Zero' in mathematics?" He asked with his blazing eyes pointing towards me.

"If you pass in examinations, this year, I would take a holy dip in the Ganges with pride" He added further turning the angry face towards me.

Everybody was silent. Dadu looked at me. But, like a defeated lawyer; he had nothing to defend against me.

I was silent too and pretended to be a victim. It was quite a stressful time having dinner.

In the morning, my mother woke me up to say:

"Somebody is calling you outside. Have you booked an auto-rickshaw?"

I quickly opened the gate to see Hari waiting for me outside my home, riding on a yellow and black coloured auto-rickshaw. His eyes were still confident, just as I saw in the class.

"Sir, please have a ride with me for this whole day." He offered me with due respect.

For a student of my calibre, getting respect from anyone was quite rare. I was quite overwhelmed by his gesture.

"Thanks, Hari," I said.

"Do you own this auto-rickshaw? Can you drive it? Is this your livelihood?" I showered many questions as such, as I got into the auto-rickshaw.

"No! I just hired to make my both ends meet" he replied to me in a confident tone.

We rode to the Kala bazaar. It was fully deserted. No trace of passengers was evident except for the Pigeons that were busy having their breakfast alongside the large Shivaji statue.

I was trying to learn a bicycle at this age and he was riding an auto-rickshaw with full control and confidence. "Shame on you, Ron!" I thought for a while.

"The day you begin scolding your conscience for something better, you get matured." Dadu had said once.

"Sir, please come and sit with me. I will tell you the basics of marketing." Hari invited me.

"Why did you stop here?" I questioned him impatiently.

"For the passengers, sir!" He replied in a slow tone.

"Here comes our first metro. The street will get crowded within fifteen minutes" He glanced at the Kala bazaar metro station staircase.

"How did you know about this?" I questioned him again.

"Experience, sir! I knew every hotspot location that could fetch me a sound business.

People transit from here to the outskirts of the city for business" He replied.

I didn't even know the way from my home to school and back. He knew everything about the district hotspot locations viable for the business. Every lane was familiar to him. "What am I familiar to?" I asked to myself.

Cheatsheet of video games, tricks to blackmail parents for the pocket-money etc., and there comes a list of 'just nonsense'." Would it help me and my parents in any way?" My conscience reverted with a strict 'No'.

"Don't call me 'sir', Hari! I told him with respect. My proudness of being a lad from a respectable family had dwindled away by now.

"You are a way ahead of me in every aspect," I told him.

I could find a rare surprise in his eyes. He was silent, still trying to understand my words.

Hari's first customer came:

"How much for Hudson Street?" A young lady asked him, applying red lipstick simultaneously. She looked more inclined towards her make-up.

"Only Rs.300 ma'am" Hari replied at once.

"Rs. Two hundred would be enough" the lady replied in a loud voice as if we were about to rob her.

Hari denied her without a thought.

"Why did you deny the offer?" I asked him out of curiosity.

"She was just checking the fare. Her face doesn't seem to be interested in riding on my Auto. Moreover, the peak hour of the business is nearing. We would get better offers to negotiate within half an hour."

After fifteen minutes, we got our customer to Hudson Street for Rs.300. He looked like a busy businessman. He didn't even negotiate for the fares.

 I saw that Lady riding with his boyfriend on a bike, from the left side mirror. "Hari was right about that lady." I thought to myself.

"How do you read people's face?" I asked him with a surprise.

"Face is the index of mind, sir!" He replied.

"Only ten per cent of customers of her age group sit in our auto-rickshaw. The probability of hiring me by a girl is very rare. Her face did not show any hurriedness. She was calm and relaxed. She looked more interested in her make-up." Hari enlightened me further while having full concentration on driving.

At his age, I didn't even know the finances at my home. He knew everything about his business.

We halted at the busy market and enjoyed the street food. He pinpointed the decent shops at the local market for shopping.

He knew almost everyone in the market. I shopped at a fifty per cent discount. Hari was like a discount coupon standing by my side.

"He is my cousin brother; so charge a reasonable price," He told every shopkeeper that I came across.

The total wages of the day was Rs.1700. He didn't look satisfied at all. He stopped at a lane and gave Rs. 500 to the auto-rickshaw owner.

Later, he distributed equal amounts from Rs. 1200 into the three piggy banks placed at the left side of the auto-rickshaw cabinet.

"The left one was for my sister's education and marriage. The right one was for the family's savings. The centre one is for me. I wanted to buy an auto – rickshaw of my own." He told me proudly.

I was in a different world. I felt a bit ashamed too. I always complain to my parents about lesser pocket money.

"Let's go home," He said.

"I have to attend a cigarette shop run by my mother to relieve some of her burden. We had a knack to shifting multiple roles to feed ourselves" He told me.

I entered his house. It was a small room, just larger than my kitchen. The bed occupied half of it. The left side housed a small cigarette shop facing the street road.

We sat there and discussed about life. I was also jotting important points for my project report.

I saw the children playing in the street barefoot and climbing on the debris. One girl of nearly eight years of age was holding another baby — lesser the age, more the responsibilities here. No amenities touched their life. I tried selling some cigarettes to the customers but failed.

Hari was quite adept in customer handling business. He called people from the streets and tried to offer his services. He knew everything about the product he was selling. I was surprised at his marketing skills.

"What else could you sell Hari?" I asked anxiously

"I can even sell the Taj mahal, if permitted." He giggled.

Ron's Best Gifts ever – samar deep singh

 Strange confidence was booming out of his eyes. His eyes had a vision and passion to succeed. For him, every second of his life was a struggle to get out of the clutches of poverty and hunger.

"What's your aim, Hari?" Another question popped up spontaneously from my mind.

"My father died of excessive drinking. But my uncle, he moved away from here and bought a nice flat in a respectable colony with his hard work. So, I want to be like my uncle." He said.

"I had everything, but yet unclear about my aims," I thought for a second.

Late in the evening, he drove me to school. We attended the evening class. He attempted all the questions of maths. But, He was quite weak in English.

Later, he dropped me at my house. I insisted him for dinner.

Dadu greeted him with respect and appreciated his efforts. I was surprised to know that he was the one who encouraged Hari to join the evening classes at my school.

He had dinner with my family. My father was very much impressed by him. I feared that he might not ask me the multiplication tables at his presence.

A few cultural lessons for me, at last. He touched everyone's feet to show respect.

I was damn sure that I would get some cultural lessons from my parents, the next day.

"You are a Genius, Hari! I am not even a chunk of your character. I was wasting my father's hard-earned money. I would set it right by working hard from now on.

You don't need a degree. You will surely succeed one day" Those words of encouragement were straight from my heart.

"No wonder! A tea seller is the prime minister of India" I thought for a while.

He smiled and left. Indeed, I have got a new friend.I gazed myself at the mirror that Dadu gave me as a gift earlier. I summoned some confidence like that of what Hari had.

"I will work hard and achieve success one day!" I promised myself.

14. The secret of the smiling Mirror

31st March 2004

The last day of March always come with unforgettable experiences in my life. As always, on this day; my class teacher handed over the report cards to every student of the class.

It's an invitation to the upcoming bad days of my life at home. The climatic fervour at my home in March used to get very much disturbed due to this damn thing.

Math had always been a headache for me. Other subjects are equally monstrous. My skills got reflected in the report card as well.

Two double zeroes in three subjects! I wonder why the teachers affix two zeroes if only one could make sense. The sum of all the subjects didn't even sum up to one subject's maximum marks. The report card was the key to an impending disaster at my home.

If only, my father could sign it blindly! No way! He's a CA. He even doesn't spare the last three digits after the decimal in his calculations. Any solution to my woes seemed a remote possibility.

I reached home with a heavy heart. Suddenly, an idea cracked my mind.

I have seen my father using correction pen nicknamed as 'the whitener', to correct errors in his calculations.

I went to his room as a spy. Quickly, I opened his cupboard,

 kept the correction pen into my pocket and rushed to my room.

Now, the calculations from my side had started. The great son of a C.A. will change the course of his own destiny. I marked one ahead of the two zeroes.

Now, I understood why teachers used to add two zeroes. It was just to facilitate such a transformation with ease. After that, I converted a miserable 33 to 93. "Pen is really mightier than the sword!" I thought a bit. It passed me with distinction without indulging into bloodshed and all the more, in a peaceful means.

Just then, there was a knock at my door. I quickly completed my remaining task and put the report card and the correction pen under the pillow.

It was my mother. "Did you get your Report card? Your father was asking about that." She asked gently.

"Yes, dear mother!" I replied.

"Then show it to your father. He is waiting for you in his room" my mother said it in a heavy tone.

I could understand the feelings of a cock at the meat shop, waiting for his turn to get butchered. "The whole world is nasty" I presumed.

Meanwhile, I presented the report card to my father. Every father is aware of the abilities of his child. I was not an exception.

"You have got 193 marks out of 100. So intelligent! Should I call you a child prodigy or a fool?" He became furious.

He threw the report card in anger onto my face.

Well, it was the blunder that I had committed. In haste, I added another one to 93 that was originally 33; when my mom entered the room.

I understood in advance. It's the time of a thunderstorm at my house.

Ten slaps back to back on my plump cheeks with a flurry of scolding and free advice for future. Even the dustbin in my house had more respect than me. I thought for a while

It seems that my Father always considered me as his favourite football; he himself being the penalty shooter. I thought for a while, caressing my plump red cheeks.

Most of the time, Dadu catches me safely in his hands as an excellent goalkeeper. Well, this is a universal truth for all the kids. I decided to find my goalkeeper to get out of the grim situation.

Two days had elapsed! Yet, the situation remained worse in the house.

Last night, at dinner; the report card saga had already been told to Dadu.

He was silent.

"Ok. I will talk to Ron!" Dadu told my father.

Sleeping with parents in such a situation was not a good idea and not even in my room. Yesterday, I had a dream of my father coming to my room and beating me ruthlessly in frustration. So, I switched to Dadu's room to be on the safer side.

"Dadu, I am sorry" I was just trying to set a stage for a good relation and a nice sleep with him.

"Have you said sorry to your father?" He asked.

"No!" I replied.

"Do you know the story of a boy with a magic mirror?"

"No!" I said in surprise.

"It's ok. Then listen, I will tell you" He turned to my side.

Once upon a time, a boy named 'Titu' was in the same situation as you are in today.

His teachers call him 'Mr. Miserable'. His classmates used to make fun of him. His studies were also in a grim state, just like that of yours. He was in an extreme state of depression.

He had no friends and no likeness towards anyone except for the famous magician of the town. People nicknamed him as 'Jadu'.

One night, at a magical fair in the city, Jadu was also a performer. Titu attended the fair and was fascinated by Jadu's performance as usual.

 The magician came to meet him after the show.

"Hello, Titu! How are you?" Jadu asked him with a wide smile.

Titu hasn't showed any warmth to his response. He was still very sad.

"Jadu! I am all alone here and a big failure too." He hugged him with tears in his eyes.

Titu's plight was unbearable to the magician.

"I have my deepest sympathies to your every concern" Jadu replied.

"I would like to give you something that may help you to overcome your grief in your life." He opened the bag and gave him a shiny gold plated mirror.

"Oh! It's very nice. But how would it help me?" Titu asked him in surprise.

"It's not an ordinary mirror, just try to see your face into it," the magician asked him.

The mirror projected the same grief on his face as he was in.

"Now try to smile," the magician said.

Titu smiled. But, the mirror presented him the same sad look as he was in earlier.

"So, my dear friend; try good things as much as you can in your life every day. Keep watching your face every night in this magic mirror. If it projected your smile, it would depict that you are improving enough and doing better in your life. The more you try to make it smile, the more sadness will leave your life." The magician explained him with a smile.

"One day, when you smile a little at the mirror and the mirror projects it as if you are laughing your heart out; That will be the best day of your life. You will keep attaining success in your life from then." He enlightened him further.

Next day; at school, he quarrelled with his classmates. Titu came home and threw his bag on the floor in anger. He slept after some time.

Next day, the alarm clock rang up at 5 o'clock sharp.

Titu got the mirror and projected his smiling face in the mirror.

The mirror showed the same sad look.

"What could I do to make it smile?" He thought to himself and slept later on.

Next day, Titu went to school. It was a normal day for him. He didn't indulge in any petty fights with his classmates. On the way, Titu helped an old lady to cross the road safely.

He came home and casually took the mirror into his hands and projected a smile again.

Titu got surprised this time.

The magic mirror had projected a little smile. But, after a few minutes, it showed him the same sad look again. He wanted to make that mirror laugh in sync with him. His urge to project a broader smile in the mirror grew even stronger.

It was another pleasant morning. Titu had a plan for this day. He woke up at 5 o'clock and went for a walk. He reached the school in time and attended every lecture with attention.

He came home and rested himself for an hour. That day, he completed all his homework and even studied for three hours. At night, he opened his bag to get that mirror.

The mirror gave him a little wider smile than that of the previous day. The mirror's increasing smile encouraged him to do something more special.

Next day- it was his birthday.

 On the note of his birthday's special speech at the school, he said sorry to the class teacher and his classmates for every mistake he had done earlier. He promised that he will behave nicely and he will never fight with anyone from then on.

In the evening, he distributed sweets to the underprivileged kids around the slum, opposite to his home and even shared the cake with all of them.

At night, he got the mirror from his bag. He saw his face into the mirror and it projected a little wider smile again.

He was quite happy but grew impatient. "When will the mirror project my complete smile?" He thought. Yet! He continued with his time-table, as planned and carried on the good work.

One day, on the way back home from his school. He saw a school bus blazing in flames. Inside the bus were many school children crying for help.

He immediately called the fire station, ambulance and the police - station from a nearby phone booth.

He opened the door of the bus with the help of the driver. He ran right through the bus corner and helped three children come out from the blazing bus.

Next day, it was another pleasant morning. But, he found himself at the city's hospital.

"So, you woke up!" He heard the nurse near his bed say.

"Where am I? Sister!" He questioned her in a low tone.

"You have got a few burns around your leg and face. But, don't worry, it would be healed with time." She replied to him.

The head doctor came and asked for his well–being.

Titu asked the doctor as to how long would it take for him to heal up his burns and wounds.

He assured him that he would help him heal as early as possible. "You have a brave and pure heart" - the doctor patted & appreciated him as well. Next evening, his class teacher and the principal came to see him.

"Great work, son!" The principle also patted him.

"You have been nominated for the president's medal for bravery," The class teacher told Titu.He smiled a little and thanked both of them.

That night, He opened his school bag to search for the mirror. To his surprise! Even before he could smile, the mirror projected a wider smile.

Later, he laughed his heart out and the mirror projected the same. Dadu concluded the story.I was very much impressed by the story.

"How could I get that mirror?" I enquired to Dadu.

"We all have that mirror inside of us." He told me with a smile on his face. I was surprised.

"It was our soul. It warns all of us if we do something bad." He enlightened me.

"Yes! My inner self had warned me while I was editing my marks with the correction pen." I said.

"And appreciates us, when we do the right things." Dadu Continued.

"It's right, Dadu! I felt elated when I helped Sam, a poor classmate, to buy a Science Textbook. I remember having self-satisfaction by my own act" I told him further.

"That's true, Ron! Never confront your inner voice. Follow your soul and that works as your smiling mirror" Dadu told me.Next morning, I went to my father and asked him for forgiveness.

My father smiled at me and advised me further not to repeat such mistakes.

I was relieved. My inner self was smiling now, that had projected on my bright smiling face.

15. A best friend for lifetime

My mommy-alarm will not be at service tomorrow to wake me up. She was diagnosed with viral fever. Her, waking me up begins with kind prayers and gradually tends to threatening words and sometimes ends with a slap.

To overcome the situation of getting up early, I had set up ten alarms to five o'clock in the morning. But, none of them were capable enough to wake me up, even after snoozing for multiple times. The school bus would arrive at 7 AM sharp and would depart exactly after five minutes wait.

That day, Dadu woke me up just twenty minutes before the bus time.

"Don't you have a bit of discipline? The clocks must have two hands to slap you, apart from the sound and snooze to wake you up; in the morning." He yelled at me.

This was enough to wake me up. I packed whatever I could possibly find necessary for the school and left home to catch the bus. I picked up the tie, socks, shoes and shoe- polish in my hands and ran after the bus that was about to depart.

I dressed up the rest in the bus, ignoring the surprised eyes of all other students.

One student at my left side asked "Did you bathe today? You are smelling bad!"

"Actually, I bathed for a longer time today, for which I got late. Please check the smell from your own or around" I told the boy and ignored him after that.

The bus assistant was gazing at me, curiously though.

"We will arrange a change-room at the extreme corner of the bus for you." He said sarcastically and laughed out aloud.

"No, thanks." I told him with an irritated expression.

In the evening, I came back to my room after the tuitions.

The burden of homework had become a nuisance for me. I made an excuse of fever and shared the photograph of clinical thermometer showing 102 degree on my family social media group. Well, it was dipped in a cup of hot tea.

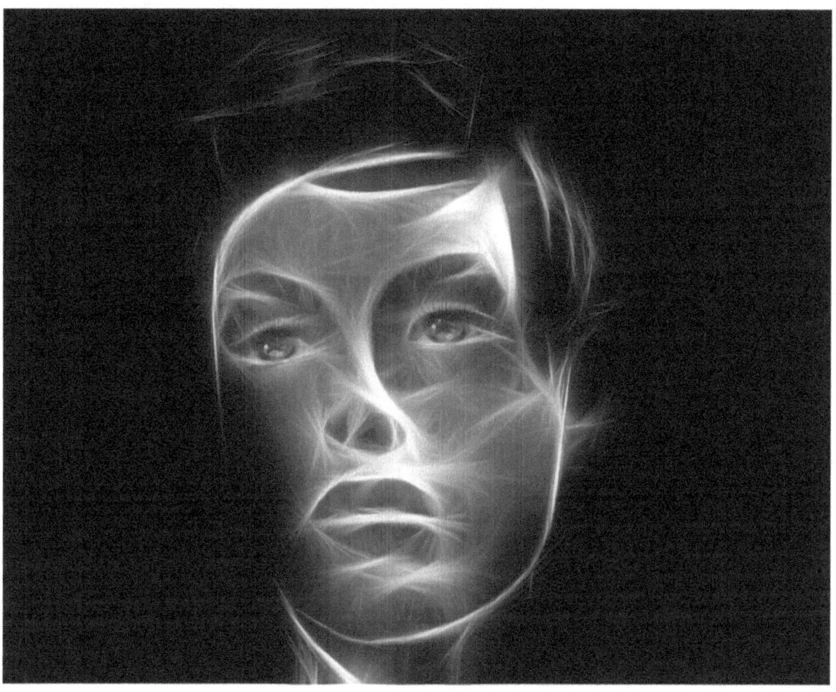

My father was smart enough. He replied to the notified messages by the class teacher that your son frequently missed the homework deadlines.

I woke up late in the next morning, after my father's office time to ensure any possible eye-contact between the two arch-rivals.

I approached Dadu's room and sneaked through the half-opened door.

He was chanting a sanskrit shloka.

No weapons can cut the soul into pieces, nor can it be burned by fire; nor moistened by water, nor withered by the wind.

Bhagavad gita 2.23

The monsoon had just arrived in North India. A frog had already peeped into his room. It was looking at Dadu, as if it has come to some rehabilitation center and asking for shelter.

"Why do you chant sanskrit shlokas in the morning?" I asked him after he finished his chants.

"It purifies the mind and keeps me calm and focussed for the whole day" - He replied in a soft tone.

"All of my friends are out of town." I informed him ignoring the lesson.

"Alas! I wish I could have a friend to talk to!" I said with a sorrowful face.

"Ron, I am heading for a short trip to the Defence academy to meet one of my old friend. I could help you to find a lifetime friend there. You have met him earlier too." He said.

"Sure, I will come with you." I jumped in joy.

After two hours of drive, we reached the heavily guarded military academy.

I was excited, but really couldn't remember any such childhood friend there.

We showed our ID cards and entered the premises.

A heavily built man with long moustache welcomed us.

"Major Vikram Rathore! You haven't changed a bit. Ha! Ha! Ha" Both embraced each other warmly.

My eyes were still wandering around, in search of a friend that Dadu told me about. "Will he hug me or not?" I questioned myself.

"We will meet like strangers. But, we will definitely make a bond thereafter just like that of my Dadu and his friend". I thought for a while.

"I'm absolutely fine and quite busy in training cadets these days." Major said with a proud smile.

"Let's have a cup of tea." He invited us further.

We stopped near a park that was initially designed for a football playground but was remodeled into a training ground for cadets. The cadets were busy in practicing various drills.

At my far left side; a series of ropes were hanging to a raised platform. Cadets were going up through those ropes to reach the raised platform; then they were jumping into a pool on the ground with a splash sound from the platform. Their speed and agility was awesome.

A guard came to us and whispered a message to the major.

"Sorry, Guys, It would take half an hour, an emergency stuff. Please excuse me" - He said and left.

"Ron! Would you like to perform that rope and platform drill?"

I thought for a while and said 'yes', reluctantly.

"Dadu, but you have to close your eyes, lest I should lose my concentration." I told him.

"Ok, sure." He said with a smile.

I went to the drill area and poured some water all over my body and came back to him.

"See! I have completed the drill" I said in a confident tone.

"Hmm! without a splash sound? You are such a genius" He added.

Meanwhile, the major came carrying some files with him.

Ron's Best Gifts ever – samar deep singh

"Breaking news! Ron has completed the platform and rope drill within two minutes and without a splash sound" Dadu told him as if he knew my bluff.

The major got surprised. "Even my trained cadets take five minutes to complete the drill. Let's see it again!" The major said.

I tried to evade the scenario but he insisted on the drill repetition. Moreover, confronting a heavy built man was not a good idea. I thought that time.

Two of his cadets also came and the Major had lined me up with them for the drill.

The major commanded us in a high pitched voice.

"You, the great soldiers of my nation; will you perform this drill for the motherland?"

We reverberated into a big 'Yes sir'.

We ran towards the rope and clinched it to reach up to the raised platform. Two of them uttered in a high pitched sound – 'Long live the mother land!'

I repeated after both of them.

Three peculiar splash sounds were heard. Mine at the last. Thanks to my NCC classes.

I came straight to Dadu and gave him a big Salute.

"Now, I heard the splash" He said with a smile.

 I confessed my bluff to Dadu shy fully and he smiled.

"Have you met your friend Ron?" Dadu asked.

I looked at him with a question mark on my face.

"At first, you disguised your soul, not to complete the drill. Later on, you gathered courage or maybe got some inspiration to complete the drill with full energy and enthusiasm." He said.

"Yes, of course! My soul got inspired by Major's words. I could never forgive myself, if I had not performed that drill along with those two cadets."

"So, you got your best friend!" He exclaimed with a smile.

"Your soul is your best friend and will remain so forever" He added further.

"The more you command it for betterment in your life, the more success you will achieve. So, love it and command it to get the best results "He enlightened me further.

Next, I performed numerous drills with the cadets. The drill with sniper dog was one of the toughest.

"Good work my son. I am proud of you." Dadu added.

In the evening, Dadu led me to the martyr's memorial inside the military academy campus. At its Centre, a list of soldiers were engraved on the pillar. He glanced at No. 102.

It read as: "No. – 102 Iqbal khan s/o Faiz khan martyred in action in 1962 war."

He grew sad. "He was my best friend" Dadu informed me.

He fought during the Indo-china war. From his childhood, we knew him as a coward and a weak child. But he wronged us by fighting with valor at the battlefield. He blew the enemy's tank single-handedly.

"Ron! The greatest honor on this earth is to sacrifice your life for the Motherland ".He enlightened me.

I got a bit emotional at this. Patriotism is such an extreme feeling.

We left the military academy and bade 'Jai Hind' to the major.

Now, it was three of us. Dadu, Me and my soul; the best friend for lifetime.

On the rear mirror of the car, I gazed myself. "Dear friend, let's work towards achieving success." I said to my soul.

PEBBLES (Round & coloured)
The Fifth Gift

My life is full of mistakes. They're like
Pebbles that make a good road.

- Beatrice wood

16. The handshake that changed the world

17. Embrace the Santa

18. Short-lived sculptures

19. Memories

16. A Handshake that changed the world

It was a compulsory extra class taken by our principal. The topic was about child rights. She had enlightened us towards our rights with finesse. Some of the rights that had grabbed from the lecture were -

Right to protection from abuse, neglect, exploitation and discrimination.

Right to proper health care services and adequate standards of living etc.

It fuelled a rebel in me. I was quite sure from the lecture that most of the rights were not given to us. The home was the first casualty. I found myself as a victim too, mostly at my home.

I came home and complained about the matter to my father. He got my right ear and led me towards my Dadu's room.

"He is asking about the rights! Tell him about his duties first. Don't you know about your marks?" He said in a loud voice. He further scolded me heavily in the presence of Dadu.

The principal had also uttered the word 'duty' that I missed. A tight slap from my father had helped me to recollect it again.

Nevertheless, my father had left the room. Dadu consoled me a bit. I asked him about the child rights during his era.

"We were unaware of anything like this. The teachers can beat us anytime and whenever they desire. They always carry a stick with them and were very strict with discipline & homework. The parent-teacher nexus was at heights in my school days. Parents used to admire the teachers, when they beat us with a stick even at our silly mistakes." Dad enlightened me about his school days.

I felt pretty lucky that I was born in this era. At least, we can talk about child rights.

"Once, I was given a punishment to write my homework multiple times, as I haven't completed it at the right time," Dadu added further.

I saw Dadu holding a paper. He was reading something.

"What were you reading?" I questioned him.

"It was a letter from one of my friend - Garfield. He hails from Poland. It was about the struggles of a boy named Percy. He's got a celebrity cult. Garfield's father found this letter from the Nazi labour camp. It was supposed to be written by Percy.

"Would you like to listen?" He asked me.

"I am all ears, Dadu," I said loudly that showed my eagerness to listen to the story in the letter.

It seems that God had left the earth since humans started to make a nuclear bomb. During that timeline, I was born. My parents called me Percy.

Poverty, impoverishment & hunger were the trademarks of my generation. Predictions of imminent World War II was looming in every heart & it was the hottest topic of the debate everywhere.

Half of the population of my village was wiped out during World War I. My home was not an exception. No medals or any sort of compensation was received, except for the hangover of loneliness & dejection to the families of the martyred soldiers.

It was another Sunday. Ten army trucks hosted their presence at my village. Every heart was awestruck with fear & despair. The future seemed bleak to every one of us.

The arrogant army officers searched our premises and investigated every member of the family in the village.

Late in the evening, all of us were crammed into the trucks.

I questioned an officer-"Why are you treating us like skeletons without a soul?"

"Don't worry, your soul would get pulled out very soon from your body" he replied arrogantly.

I got a bit terrified & came to the conclusion that the coming days would be very tough in the near future.

The trucks halted at a big building at its ruins. The periphery was strictly guarded & fenced. They housed all of us inside a big hall. It seemed that they had packed the whole village into a big hall. I could sense that every person here, was more tensed and fearsome about the future.

After two days, most of them were transported to Nazi concentration camp at Auschwitz, on the outskirts of Poland. My family was also transported here via a filthy rail freight car.

Fifteen days had elapsed; the conditions had got worse with each passing day. Maltreatment, diseases, starvation and overwork were the norms of everyday. It was the Nazi labour camp.

Only the fittest could survive here. The whereabouts of the unfit, old & lazy souls can't be questioned by the authorities. A chunk of the older population had disappeared within a week.

Only the working-age group of 15 to 40 years were left behind. It was the only reason that my family was still united. A sixteen-hour of day's work was rewarded by a filthy bowl of soup & a single loaf of bread each night.

A minute mistake at work would mean a handsome gift of twenty lashes irrespective of age and gender. I reckoned that the human rights were meant for only the rich and royal families. Our presence had no meaning on this earth.

At the advent of the nuclear age, God was the first casualty. It seemed that the age of the devil had arrived. Within a month, the whole camp was struck with disease and utmost miseries of human life.

"Even the hell must have some standards" my mother used to utter in a low voice.

Apparently, we had become slaves of a siren. It dictated our time-table & hence our luck.

Despite all of this; I had a special privilege at that damn premises.

I made friend with a guard, who allowed me to stand near the fence, late in the evening. He warned me not to touch the fences as those were made of electrified barbed wires. Watching some activity outside, though it was a deserted place; gave me some respite from the hell inside.

One day, my parents had contracted with diarrhoea. Two male doctors came to diagnose them. My parents refused to take any treatment or diagnosis. They were willing to work diligently despite the disease. But, the doctors stood firm for the follow-up treatment. They took my parents to a cell, deep inside the hall.

I wondered why my parents had refused the medical services.

Three weeks had passed.I couldn't dare to ask anyone about the well-being of my parents. They didn't return. One day, I have seen a lorry carrying clothes of my parents. The driver wore my father's engagement ring. Since then, all my hopes about their return got dashed.

I was assigned the work of cleaning the pathways alongside the fences. At times, I watched a wagon that halted for an hour. It unloaded all its goods & departed afterwards from the camp. It was a heavily guarded & secretive activity.

I was pretty sure that the wagon was meant to unload something precious and of utmost importance. Respect for human labour was quite scarce in the industrial era.

The wagon had embossed a letter 'W' on its sides & back with two circles crossing each other. My eyes remained glued to that wagon; until it departed.

  Meanwhile, I had developed a hobby of engraving anything with a sharp iron wedge on the stones lying at the fences; as a time pass measure.

On one particular day, the siren, which became friendly to all of us, had rung up. It announced that the delegates of the Red Cross society were coming to inspect the premises.

We, all have to maintain discipline & show some decent behaviour. We have to present ourselves happy & content in front of the committee members.

A long list of Do's & Don'ts were given to us. In the evening, a piece of black forest cake was also served to all of us.

The delegation had four members. One boy with plump cheeks also accompanied them. He was the son of the chief executive head of the committee. They inspected the whole premises & took some samples of the food. I was standing at the fence when they were about to depart. I have seen that the guards & officers were exchanging pleasantries with each other.

The boy, out of curiosity came to me. He smiled a bit & asked about my well - being.

I was aware that the guard above the roof was watching us. A warm handshake was made between me the the boy. A little smile was exchanged in return, from my side.

"Hello, folk! I am Garfield. Are you here with your parents?" He asked me in a soft tone.

I remained silent. I was well aware of the fact that the price of friendly talk with the boy would get much costlier after his departure.

I gave him three pieces of engraved stones. Garfield kept it quickly into his pocket. The guard looked suspicious but took no strange notice."

"Dadu paused for a minute. It was all from Percy" He added.

"How Percy had got celebrity status?" I asked Dadu impatiently.

He told me further.

"It was the heroic and keen observation of that father-son duo that made Percy- a Hero.

"Dad! See what the boy at the labour camp had given me? Three stones with nice engravings. The first one was so beautifully engraved." Garfield told his father curiously.

"Let me see. It was a symbol of an old military facility that I had visited ten years ago. It was shut as per our records." Garfield's father answered his curious son.

"Then, how would have the boy come to know about that premises symbol? He was around ten, just about my age. I am sure that he wanted to give us some important message." Garfield reverted to his father.

His father's curiosity about the symbol engraved on the stone had encouraged Garfield to discover the meaning of the other two.

Another stone with an engraved symbol had a plough with a numeral twenty – one and three stars marked on the left side.

Garfield insisted his father to release a postal ticket having the image of that symbol.

It was done promptly without any delay by his father.

The third stone engraving was quite easy to understand. It had a Dove holding a handkerchief at its beak.

It seemed that it was tried to colour the handkerchief in white with chalk. It was the message of peace, quite easy to understand.

Garfield told his father about it that convinced him too.

After six months, a handicapped soldier in rags came to his father at home; holding a post-card with the same postal ticket affixed at the left corner bearing the symbol of second engraved stone.

"How have you got the idea of this symbol?" He asked Garfield's father very politely

"The numeral twenty one denoted my house number & the three stars depict my district logo. My grandfather engraved the same symbol at the exit door." He enlightened Garfield's father, furthermore.

Garfield understood the whole scenario & told everything he knew to the soldier about Percy.

The soldier became sad. He was the elder brother of Percy, whom Garfield had met earlier.

Meanwhile, the investigations about the first symbol took almost a year to get it deciphered.

One day Garfield's father came home & hugged him.

"We have deciphered the symbol," He told him happily.

"It was a top-secret defence facility engaged in making bombs & armaments for the upcoming war by the Nazis. It housed a nuke research facility at the same premises too. The labour camp was a secret warehouse to store these weapons of war. We have also found two trucks with the same 'W' symbol engraved on its sideways." He said.

"With the help of our armed forces, we have captured all the weapons from the labour camp & destroyed the Nazi defence facility. That boy at the labour camp had helped us to unearth a major weapon arsenal. The Nazi armed forces were planning for a major attack on our city. Percy saved millions of lives." Garfield's father told him.

"A mere handshake had foiled a major enemy attack." Garfield thought for a while.

"Have you got any trace of Percy, at the labour camp?" Garfield asked his father, curiously.

"We found nothing there, except a mass grave and a letter. It must be written by Percy. I am very sorry for him." Garfield's father replied sadly.

"Please send this letter to Percy's elder brother." Garfield requested his father.

After a short while, Garfield's father shared Percy's story & the letter to the media. He had become a celebrity since then. He saved the whole city from war. A memorial was erected for him, which was inaugurated by the President himself. At its bottom, the replica of three stones with the same three symbols engraved was erected.

It was written at the bottom:

"Yes to peace & family! No to war ".

"I have no words to say anything about the sacrifice of that boy". I told him, being a bit sad about Percy.

"Rights are important, but the duties must be complied seriously," Dadu added further.

I took out the three coloured pebbles from my pocket that I had collected from the river stream earlier, similar to that of Dadu's given pebbles. I engraved three words on them with a sharp tool.

It read ---- Peace, family & No war. The three most important timeless words of any era of human civilization.

17.Embrace the Santa

The Christmas that had passed a week ago was very special to

me. I was given the responsibility to decorate my house. I had chosen the theme 'red' along with the liberal use of Red LED lights outside my home & on the bushes. I had also ordered an artificial 'Christmas tree' from an online store & decorated it with ornaments and stars.

Also, a handmade Christmas wreath for the first time was hung at the front door to welcome the guests. An artificial snowman & an inflatable Santa were also adorned outside the house to welcome the Santa & guests around the Christmas week.

That Christmas night, Dadu came to my room dressed in a Santa attire & presented me a gift.

"What about the other gifts in the bag?" I asked him.

"They are the gifts for some special children that struggle to meet their both ends meet. Would you like to come with me?" He proposed.

"I would love to come with you," I told him excitedly. I assured him that I would wrap all the gifts for him next time.

He drove to the street that led to the nearby slum of our area. He distributed the gifts to the poor children there. Some of the children insisted him to tell a story.

We sat at a park around a banyan tree. He began to tell us another story.

Once upon a time, Santa was deputed to keep the world in order. He was a jovial young man in his prime thirties. The kingdom of Gomes was a happy place to live. It was quite a calm & peaceful place amidst the valley surrounded by the mountains. People believed in the existence of God & his Deputy Santa was loved & revered by everyone.

The Gospel of Christ was scripted in edicts at every nook and corner of the kingdom and were strictly adhered to.

Every last day of the month, Santa wore a red coat having white fur collar and cuffs, a white fur cuffed red trousers, a red hat & reddish-brown boots. He carried a bag full of gold coins, which got replenished the same night every time, the coins were distributed.

He came to the countryside & kept singing through the streets he visited:

"Whoever will toil harder, he will get the larger share of the gold coins from Santa's bag".

Santa was the sole representative to distribute the gold coins in the villages of the kingdom of Gomes. He used to distribute it to the farming heads of the family as per the monthly production at the farms. The farmers toil very hard at the orchard farms in the hope that Santa would reward them handsomely.

But, not every household in the kingdom was happy. Some of the citizens were not so hardworking & honest. They kept a covetous eye on Santa's bag. They wished to snatch the whole bag; that would make them rich at once.

Most of such unscrupulous citizens tried to become Santa's disciple, to know the secret of the bag. They were quite jealous of the larger share that the hardworking people received. The people who got a lesser share were also not content. They preached for the equality which was turned a deaf ear by the Santa & the king too.

The king didn't interfere with Santa's work. He had a belief that his citizens will remain honest & religious as long as Santa is there.

The church at St. Cathedral was the Santa's residence. It was a pious & most venerated venue in the whole kingdom. It sat proudly at the monumental base, designed in mighty Byzantine architecture. The interior & exterior was set in grey sandstone marble. The floor was paved with alternate white & black squared tiles.

A conspiracy was planned to steal the gold coins from the bag right from the heart of the church. A gang of robbers went inside the St. Cathedral church to search for the bag. The gold coins heist was quite successful. The robbers stole a huge sum of gold coins.

Confident with this success, some unscrupulous citizens had also organized themselves into groups to perform another feat of robbery without any fear. Everybody knew that the Gold coins would get replenished every time it had been taken out.

A year had passed. The cases of robbery in the church had increased manifold. The respect & craze of Santa had diminished a lot. People also grew lazy with time & no one wanted to work hard at the orchard farms. Everyone thought of an easy way to heist gold coins from the church.

Farm produce had also suffered a lot. A chunk of citizens had even refused to collect any Gold coins from Santa. A time had come that if anyone needed money; that person only had to barge into the church & steal the Gold coins. In due course of time, the economy of the state had got paralyzed.

Meanwhile, Santa grew sad by the thefts in the church premises. But, he was so kind-hearted that he had never complained about the cases of the theft to the king. He had decided to take some steps so that the theft cases could stop.

Santa deputed six elves to stop the theft cases; in each direction of the church to catch the thieves.

The zigzag pathway at the church confused the elves. Moreover, the robbers had learnt to misled them easily.

Knowing that the elves were deputed at the church premises, the gang of thieves performed theft in unison & with utmost precision.

They planned varied smart ways to overcome the situation. Once, the gangs deputed some members just to guise the elves, while others sneaked in to search the bag. Some of the gangs dressed their members in black with painted black face to camouflage the elves at night.

Next, Santa decided to use the power of his magic spells to stop the theft cases at the church premises.

He cast a magical spell that whoever will enter the church at night will get blinded inside the church premises only; so that no one could trace the bag full of gold coins.

With time, the theft cases lessened in number. Santa had a sigh of relief.

After six months, the theft cases had risen again. Also, the visitors at day time had risen enormously at the church premises. The gang of robbers in the guise of appreciating the sculptured walls of the church & the architecture had mapped & calculated it's every nook & corner.

There was a sudden spurt of art lovers for the church architecture. Some of them took the whole day to appreciate the beauty & splendour of the church. Santa cast his suspicious eyes on them. But, he couldn't do anything due to the lack of evidence.

The thieves marked every location of the church by touching the nook & corner of the church.

They even calculated & rehearsed at daytime, the number of steps taken to reach the rooms of the church. In due course of time, the theft cases had risen exponentially.

Another spell was cast by the Santa that was to stop the ability to hear at the church premises at night. In addition to that, talking to each other & gathering to praise the architecture inside the church premises was strictly forbidden at daytime.

Other previous spells were also equally applied. It would stop the communication between the thieves & they can't even map the church premises as well.

Now, Santa was confident that the theft cases would diminish at the church premises.

The thieves devised another way to overcome this situation. Whenever Santa came to the village to distribute the gold coins, they showed undue respect & warmth to him. They used to thank him by gifting marigold flowers.

Some of them even rubbed the marigold flowers at the bag surface. Others smeared scent at the bag without his notice so that the smell could be retained for a long time. Thieves sneaked into the church for theft thereafter. They desperately searched for the smell of scent and marigold flowers inside the church premises.

There was a considerable spurt in the theft activities again, inside the church premises.

Finally, Santa consulted the king. He also advised him that any harsh methods or punishments should not be employed.

So, after a week; on an auspicious day, a grand ceremony at the church was held. Santa gave away the bag to the king. The king even vowed that the bag would not to be used again.

The king also announced economic reform measures at the kingdom. He started the paper currency with further reforms on law and order at the kingdom. System of courts & punishments were also to be adhered by the citizens strictly.

But, this made Santa unemployed. He wrote Christmas carols during his pastime & even increased the prayer timings. But, the boredom was prevalent in his life & it took a heavy toll on his health & happiness.

Meanwhile, a young boy entered the church premises for shelter & food with a newborn baby. The boy also begged the Santa to bless her ailing sister.

 Santa blessed both the kids. Next day, they left the church to home. Santa hugged both of them & even gave them some precious gifts. Since then, Santa started thinking about the welfare and well-being of kids in the kingdom.

One day, at late in the evening; he set out to the village to know about the well - being of the two children who visited the church a few days back.

He entered the cottage. The two kids were sleeping. He coughed in a low voice"....Ho...Ho".

Both of them woke up and the boy approached him at once. Santa asked him about his well-being. The boy was happy to meet him again. Santa promised to visit him again with the gifts.

Ron's Best Gifts ever – samar deep singh

At the countryside, Santa saw the sick children shivering with cold and sleeping on the footpaths. He grew sad. He was moved by these incidents. He went straight to the church and called upon the meeting with the elves. They discussed how they could fill the lives of the miserable children with happiness.

It was decided that the Santa will distribute gifts to the poor children at night every weekend. This will also cultivate a breed of honest & selfless citizens. The lessons of morality should start from childhood itself. He concluded at the meeting.

It was the last week of December. Once again, Santa wore a red coat having white fur collar & cuffs, a white fur cuffed red trousers, a red hat & reddish-brown boots. He carried a bag full of gifts for the poor children & set out to the village.

He blessed & distributed the gifts to the able, hardworking & underprivileged children of the kingdom.

On his return journey to the church, he saw a boy fighting with a poor girl. The boy glanced at Santa & guised himself as a victim. But Santa knew it all.He spanked him & moved ahead.

"The gifts were meant for the able, honest & hardworking children." He told the boy & left to the church. "Dadu concluded.

All the children were happy with the story. It was a bonus along with the Christmas gifts.

Back home, I opened the gift that Dadu gave me.

It was a camera along with five round & coloured pebbles and a letter.

It read:

Dear Ron!

Collect memories. The round coloured pebbles depict the collection of sweet memories in life. I know it's hard to collect round coloured pebbles from the river stream. But, nothing is impossible; if tried persistently. It's the same with our life.

Try to seize good memories from your life in whatever situation you are in. The camera will help you do it.

Love you

Dadu

18. Short – lived Sculptures

Apart from the ice cream pact with Dadu, I had other informal

protocols with my family members, neighbours & the school friends. One of them was the 'Statue protocol'. It excludes my father, the school principal & the class teacher.

I could disturb anyone by saying a word 'statue' at once in a loud tone & with the fingers of one hand in a crossed position. The recipient would have to stop his work & must stand in the same 'statue' position without any movement.

Once, I had tried this protocol with the school principal too. It got reversed.

That day she made me stand outside her office in 'statue' position with the fingers crossed. Next, I tried it with my father. I was slapped at once, rendering all my senses into 'statue' position.

Meanwhile, it worked well with the mother. Whenever she catches me in a mischief red-handedly & tried to beat or scold me, I used to say 'statue' and she would 'freeze' in a statue mode. Thereafter, she forgets my mischiefs and moves on with her household chores.

Once I sneaked in through Dadu's room. He was on the balcony.

I said 'Statue' to him.

He moved to my side." Oh, Ron! I have found a sparrow's nest in the balcony. It was broken by the wind. I was helping the sparrow to get the nest alright."

After his social service activities for the sparrow, we sat for another bedtime story in the balcony.

Here he goes!

Asmara was the art capital of Zion, the prosperous nation somewhere in the middle-east. Traders & tourists flock into the city to have a glimpse of magnificent artefacts & sculptures.

The breathtaking sculptures beautified every street of the city. Artisans were so adept & skilled that they got frequent invitations to carve out the sculptures far and wide.

Sir Becker was one of the esteemed artisans. Art lovers used to say that he adds life to his sculptures. His artwork was sold like hotcakes. But, he had a secret that was hidden from everyone.

 His sculptures come to life to serve him for some time & to acknowledge the efforts of his master. But, Mr Becker was the humble man of principles. He never sought any favour from them. He only wished good luck to his crafted master -pieces of art.

Recently, he made an old man's sculpture. It was a masterpiece in white sandstone carving. It had a toned body draped in white with curly hairs extending up to the shoulders. His eyes showed the experience of age & face looked quite tensed. His right hand was holding a scripture & the left one pointed towards the earth. He stood with one leg bearing its full weight and the other one forward. He finished it with extreme care & attention in just three weeks.

At night, when he was having rest, the old man's sculpture came to life & said thanks to him. Mr Becker humbly accepted it with a smile on his face. The old man asked for any wish he could fulfil, but Mr Becker denied him.

Within a month, he made another sculpture of a woman with a child in her lap. Her face had heavy brows and elongated nose with a distinctive mole at the left side of the cheek. The arms had slightly curved hands and slender fingers that were resting a smiling baby. A minister of parliament had ordered it. He finished it within a lesser time frame. So, he got exhausted.

One night, the women's sculpture came to life along with the child.

"Thanks master for crafting me & my baby. You looked extremely tired. Can I help you by massaging your body?" She asked him in a soft & humble tone.

But, Mr Becker was silent & did not answer the lady. He was too tired to react anymore.

The lady massaged his hands & legs gently. The child was smiling. It gave Mr Becker a slight relief but also reverberated his mind into the past memories.

"Those were heydays when my wife & child used to sit close to me. Both watched me finishing the sculptures. Now, it had become a memory of the past."

He thanked the lady & went asleep.

Mr Becker had a son. His name was John. Being very busy with his artwork, he never tried to carve his son into a gentle & humble citizen. John kept himself busy in vices of his time. He took no interest in his studies as well as in learning his father's art. At school, he had an arrogant & impulsive behaviour.

One day, the postman came to Mr Becker's art studio. It was the warning letter to get his son rusticated by the school principal & the yearly marks assessment report card of his son.

John came from school quite late in the evening. Mr Becker enquired him about the lesser marks & the rustication warning letter. But, he talked to Mr Becker rudely that had hurt him a lot.

"I have become old. You should either study hard at the school or assist me at the art studio." Mr Becker left to his room with a heavy heart.

A boy next door ordered him to sculpt three rats as a birthday gift. He sculptured them in a day. The three rat sculptures, at midnight, came to life. They went to John's room & tore his clothes into rags.

Next morning, John was confused about what had happened to his clothes.

Mr Becker kept himself busy in sculpting final touches to a warrior sculpture. The grey sandstone statue depicted a wounded warrior. A bleeding sword wound was visible at his left side of the chest. He rested on his fallen shield while his sword, belt, and a baton lie beside him.

Though busy with sculpting, Mr Becker was thinking about his son. "God, please help my child with some wisdom" He prayed in despair.

The warrior sculpture at midnight came to life & went straight to John's room. It had beaten him a lot with the baton. John was drunk. He can't recognize the person who had beaten him.

At school, John couldn't sit at the desk. His bottom had been swollen. Everyone made fun of him. He was furious & came to his father's art studio.

"Father, had you beaten me yesterday night?" The boy said nothing further as he did not want to disclose that he was drunk.

Mr Becker remained silent." I don't believe in violence or punishments." He told him after a pause. John went to his room after a while.

After some time, Mr Becker sculptured a pretty lady to perfection.

The female sculpture had a toned body draped in white & grey colour with distinct joined eyebrows. She wore a single broad necklace at the neck. She looked pretty in the white sandstone marble.

It came to life to acknowledge his master's efforts.

"Sir, I will try to get your son on the right path." She told Mr Becker.

She went to John's room & sat near his bed. She tried to wake him up gently. John opened his eyes & was surprised to see a pretty lady at his side.

He asked the lady about the cause of her arrival.

"I will come to you every night. We will discuss how you have spent the day. If you remain true to your heart, I will become the best friend of yours. If you lie to me, my each body part will turn into stone with each passing day." She said to john in a soft tone.

Later on, John boasted of his activities & great work done by him every night to the lady.

The lady knew about his lies.

She had turned herself into sculpture at last. John didn't even care for that.

"Sorry sir, I had failed. Your son had no emotions. He had a heart of stone that didn't melt even at my pain & sufferings. He is far worse than us." She told Mr Becker & turned again into sculpture.

"My lady! Best of luck for your future." Mr Becker told her & bade goodbye.

With a heavy heart, he completed another sculpture of a Priest within a few days.

 Seated in a serious attitude, he rested on the chair and one hand holding his beard. His face was shining. The draperies were in white folds.

The arms and bones of the hands were sculpted to perfection being slender but muscular. The face did not show the attributes of arrogance but seemed to contain self-confidence & rock-solid patience.

One night, the priest came to life. He saw his master in grief.

"Master, you don't worry. You look very tired. It is requested to you to go to the woods for some time & come here after a few days.

I promise that I will make your son wise & obedient. But, it is requested to make your own sculpture. I will need it." The priest told him.

 Mr Becker did the same as advised by the priest.

John came to his father's art gallery & he watched his father's sculpture in surprise.

"It is my father's replica. Who had sculpted his masterpiece?" John asked himself. He found a priest sitting in the corner of the art studio.

The priest explained that he had turned his father into a sculpture. It was his last wish. Your father had no desire to live anymore. So he requested me to transform him into a sculpture. He said that he was very disappointed with his son. He had failed him. He had no desires left to enjoy life anymore."

John grew restless. He asked the priest as to how he could bring his father back to life.

"Your father could only come to life if you can make a replica of your father's sculpture." The priest replied.

"Well, it's not possible, Mr Priest. My father was an expert artisan. How could I sculpt that same? I don't possess the requisite skills." John told the priest.

"My Dear friend, nothing is impossible. Practice makes a man perfect." He told him & left the studio. I will meet you next week.

John started making the sculpture of his father & tried his best, but he was unable to make it. The priest came & analyzed his work.

"It's a crap & not even seemed to be a joker's sculpture. You haven't grasped even a bit of your father's art." The priest was furious at him.

"Can you help me as to how I could make a perfect replica of my father's sculpture?" He prayed to the priest.

"Make sculpting as your hobby. Skill sharpens if you turn it into a hobby & passion. Add emotions & feelings in your art." The priest replied.

"I will make the deal quite easy for you as you seem desperate to meet your father. Just make your father's bust, not the whole sculpture." The priest told him & left the studio.

He rolled the clay into an oval shape. He drew three horizontal symmetrical lines at the oval shape to mark the eye-line, lip-line & nose line. A vertical line was also drawn to divide the face into half. These were the basics that he had learnt from his father at childhood.

He closed his eyes & remembered his father's plump round face. He imagined how he used to touch his father's cheeks every now & then, at childhood. He shaped the front of the oval slightly round with a spatula to shape the face.

Next day, He took a part of clay & rolled it into pyramidal shape & attached it below the eyes at the vertical line. He remembered that in his childhood, he always touched his father's nose to play with him.

It was bulbous in appearance & had a large protruding shape with a rounded curved tip that protrudes outward to create a bulbous circular mass at the bottom of the nose. He tried to carve it into the sculpture with the same pyramidal shaped clay.

He smoothened the contours of the pyramidal shape down the eye-line & rest of the oval shape. It made him happy as he gauged the first streak of success. It resembled exactly like his father's nose. It took him a whole day.

He saw his father's brow bones pointed downwards as if it didn't show any confidence due to his activities that brought a bad name to the family. He thought for a while & wept.

Later on, he added another two rolled cylinders to the oval figure & curved them downwards to attach above the eye-line. It made the brow bones below the forehead.

His father had deep-set and small eyes that were set deeper into the skull which helped him to add precision to his work.

The experience of age was visible through them that made him look confident & attractive. He thought for a while.

He gouged the eyes by the gouging tool. He remembered how he closed his father's eyes before revealing his sketches, made on his drawing book during his childhood.

He closed his eyes & acted to dab his father's cheekbones; as if he had touched his father's face. It had plum rounded, flabby & wrinkled cheeks with a dimple on the left side. He used to poke it via his index finger for fun. He took the curved spatula to carve the cheekbones with a dimple at last.

Next were the lips to sculpt. It always protruded a smile irrespective of any situation, but it got lost with time. He added curved cylinders made from clay at the lip-line to carve out the lips.

Everyone said that his lips resembled his father's. He went to the mirror & looked at his lips. He painted his lips first with colour & then kissed the mirror afterwards.

 That smeared his lip design at the mirror. He took its replica on the butter paper. He pasted them to the rolled cylinders on the oval figure & gave the cylinders into the shape of lips.

He carved two circles from the left out clay & made the ears to affix them at the eye line but sideways. His father had round ears with rounded lobes that he touched many times. He carved the details of the ears with a rounded tool.

At last, he made the bust seamless & smoothened out with a sharpening tool. Rest of the details like chin, hair & neck were made by him easily.

Afer a week, his father came to the studio along with the priest. Mr Becker's sculpture was still there. "Nice, you have learnt the art." Mr Becker said to john with a smile on his face.

"I love you, father." John hugged him at once.

" I missed you a lot." Mr Becker replied.

Now, John could be seen working at the art gallery along with his father, who was now a proud & content man.

"Dadu, I was awestruck with the story."

I remembered that Dadu had given me round pebbles on my birthday as a gift.

Once, I desperately searched for the similar coloured round pebbles. After a few days of intense visit & search, I found such pebbles at the river stream.

The trio of passion, skills and hobby could lead us to the path of success in any field.

19. Memories

25.12.2018

Mumbai

My father called me up on Christmas Eve.

"Merry Christmas son!" He wished me, but I sensed a dull enthusiasm in his voice.

"Same to you, Dad. I miss you" I responded. He smiled but grew sad after a pause.

"Your Dadu's fourth death anniversary would be on December 29. We have planned a family reunion to commemorate it." He told me with a heavy heart.

I took flight from Mumbai to Dehradun & reached early morning of the same day. I set out for a morning walk. It had been a long time; almost a decade since I had been at my home.

It was the same day as usual, but the fragrance of life was missing. Pigeons at the Lal chowk were fed regularly. Birds have their meals in my courtyard. My father continued the tradition to feed & water them regularly.

I entered Dadu's room. There was an unusual emptiness in his room.

 Another photograph was added to the photo-frames on the four walls. It was him. He looked smiling & content.

Everything changes with time. You don't know when your world would turn upside down. I thought for a while.

After all, it's about the memories. I dabbed on one of his favourite photographs. He was smiling & standing by a fighter jet aircraft. I took it into my hand & found a letter at its back.

It read:

Dear Ron!

The best part of my life was to watch you grew up. You have completed my lonely old days with pride and joy since your mother gave you into my lap. At first, you took a pee and smiled at me. I knew that you would grow up to be a naughty one. Your smiling face on my lap gave me the meaning of life.

After the death of your grandmother, I was all alone & sad. You became the reason of my life after that. You ran to me after every conflict with your parents. I liked that so much. Resolving your every issue was my priority.

It was your first day of school. You cried so much to be at home with me. So, I joined you at your school on the first day. It continued for a month until you felt familiar.

The ice cream pacts, the toss and the statue protocols to resolve any issue & enjoy the moments of life were quite awesome. You made me learn how to lead life peacefully without any conflict while being happy & content at the same time. Life was so simple. I had only imagined it after meeting you. You made me learn that after all, it's the family to be given utmost importance.

Ron, remember that it's not important to be a topper or wealthier. It's important to be a good person with a helping nature at first.

Don't forget a child within you. Keep it handy all the time.

Take selfies & enjoy life. Gather memories & make friends. Your wealth of memories must be greater than the real one.

Memories must make you smile in your tough or maybe the last days of your life.

I am again reminding you about the significance of five gifts that I had given you on your birthdays.

Hourglass:	**Respect time. It will not come back**
Magnifying glass:	**Be logical at every step**
Mirror:	**Be true to yourself**
Violin:	**Don't forget to enjoy life.**
Coloured marbles:	**Gather memories in life.**

Your beloved Grandfather

'Dadu'

"Thanks, Dadu. I owe my success to you, as the CEO of a reputed MNC at such a young age. Your gifts had shown me the way of success in my life. They have shaped my life." I thought for a while.

I found a coin near the showcase. With it, we used to toss & decide in case of any conflict. It was a great problem solver. I took it into my pocket. "Life is quite simple; don't make it complex." He said to me once, while tossing the coin.

I slept on his bed with his pillow held in my arms. After all! It's all about the memories that are left behind.

Please give your feedback

Samar1075@yahoo.com

Thanks for reading